Reuben

by

Tito Perdue

Books by Tito Perdue

Lee (1991)
The New Austerities (1994)
Opportunities in Alabama Agriculture (1994)
The Sweet-Scented Manuscript (2004)
Fields of Asphodel (2007)
The Node (2011)
Morning Crafts (2013)
Reuben (first edition, 2014)
The Builder: William's House I (2016)
The Churl: William's House II (2016)
The Engineer: William's House III (2016)
The Bachelor: William's House IV (2016)
Cynosura (2017)
Philip (2017)
Though We Be Dead, Yet Our Day Will Come (2018)
The Bent Pyramid (2018)
The Philatelist (2018)
The Smut Book (2018)
The Gizmo (2019)
Love Song of the Australopiths (2020)
Materials for All Future Historians (2020)
Journey to a Location (2021)
Vade Mecum (2022)

Reuben

by

Tito Perdue

Standard American Publishing Company
Brent, Alabama
2022

For Judy. Always and again.

Foreword

The story begins in moments from now, as soon as the aftermath arrives of something that happened one time.

Remember? How in those times we used to keep watch till night, you and I, and then come outside and climb the hill? One would have thought there was nothing to look forward to except further dimness by day and additional darkness at night and keeping steadfast vigil, you and I, from places in the home and field.

(Followed then several moments in silence.)

And how we used to trudge on down to where in old times a certain one we both remember well would wait all night with his legs dangling over the Edge as he cradled in his lap that well-remembered lizard of which the county still sometimes tells? Vehement indeed was the weather in those days, and so dense (he said) *with unorganized matter hurtling past that many times* (and I believe him) *he could have leapt across the distance and built his home upon an unclaimed star. But the rest you know—how he did one thing and another, ending up as a minor constellation in the northern sky.*

(Again, Lee fell silent. A chill was up, bringing with it the smell of unharvested apples deteriorating on the stem. He attributed it to the people who had run off in such haste toward the ever-expanding cities that now touched each other across broad distances. Working quietly, he folded the blanket more closely about the woman, uncertain whether she were sleeping or not.)

They never went about in daylight, Lee and his wife, nor set foot on land that was not their own. And because she was prone to falling unconscious and remaining that way for certain hours, he had to prod her to the hill and haul her to the summit and, gathering her head in both hands and aiming it in the right direction, describe for her ears alone the things that had come to pass in nearby counties.

"See that?"

She nodded.

"And there, did you see that? It never ends, and it never does!"

"Never. Can we go in now? The cold."

"And there!" (It seemed to him that he was seeing more than usual, and that his powers of observation were even more acute tonight than by comparison with his usual standard. He saw a lot, and what he saw told him all that he immediately needed to know about a great number of things.)

"This is why we never leave the house," he said, "except at night. And over there, that's the reason why . . ."

She agreed.

Those airplanes leaping off the tarmac? Trying to effectuate an escape. For this he blamed the boy next door, who had chosen this time for trying out his kite, a tattered item as black as the bats who served as consorts for the thing.

Remember? How we left the hill, you and I and, traveling far, came to where the surf broke like glass on what till then had been our native shore? And when as on the first day of the world we stood gazing for hours at the inordinate sun? "Because life," you said, "must someday end." Came then the light.

And I recall the boy reeling in the stars and kite, and you upon the shore, asleep when all was bright.

One

At the time of The Second Council, when thirty-seven cities had agreed to unify and a man could grow old and die without having ever smelt "the wet smell of a wet mule in wet rain," and women wanted to be like men, *that* was when large numbers began to be seen loitering on street corners wishing for life to come to an end. In such a situation as that, one could hardly blame the better sort of people for wanting to draw apart and live where census takers and others of that kind refused to follow. Some might choose to keep a cow, to give one example or, to give several, several. Or, failing in that, might prefer to toddle on down hand-in-hand to the Edge, as if the time for transferring over to other planets had not all long ago passed away. They could not know, of course, neither Lee nor his wife, that at that very moment History itself in ungainly form was broaching nigh unto their house.

Such then was the disposition of Lee and his two-person family when on the fifth day a tall and hollow-looking youth blundered in upon them from out of the hills. Groaning, Lee rose and went forward to meet him, much embarrassed to be covered up in the flour-like material with which for the past half hour he had been powdering the dog.

"Pefley," he said, extending his hand but then immediately drawing it back again when he realized that the boy was even more uncouth and unacceptably dressed than he had at first supposed. "Of the Alabama Peflies, don't you know," he went on, noting then that the fellow carried a staff that would have sufficed alike for holding dragons at bay or vaulting over valleys. Keeping his eye on that staff, Lee called for his cane, knowing full well that the woman couldn't hear him. Thus far the churl had said nothing, and meantime Lee was growing more and more appalled by his "shoes," a makeshift arrangement in which one foot was fitted out in leather and the other a sort of canvas with holes in it. Came now the boy's voice, a guttural sound asking for water. Far away Lee could see his wife running toward the house where the cane was stored.

"'Water,' he says! And yet I don't hear him offering to work for it, I just don't."

The older man led the way, a sixty-yard stroll to where some two or three cords of mixed firewood lay in an asymmetrical heap. Smiling, Lee now took the cane in one hand and the ax in the other and through a series of un-derstandable errors proceeded to offer the wrong instru-ment to the boy.

"And there's another pile behind the barn."

Dragging the ax after him, the vagrant waded into the stack and began at once to work. Encouraged by his atti-tude, Lee came chasing after, highly resolved that on this one occasion at least he'd get a decent payment in return for what had been asked of him.

"Lift high the ax," he called through cupped hands, "but when bringing it down, do it with your *strength*." Suddenly he jumped back, dodging a length of hickory so admirably split that it looked like surgeon's work. It was while he was inspecting it (turning it with his cane), that another of them—he squawked out loud—came flying out of the pile and smote him on the shank. Immediately Lee raised his cane and took two steps forward before then coming to a complete halt when he remembered how much more formidable were the ax and boy as compared to himself and the cane. And then, too, he was benefiting from the boy's energy, the sections of wood "falling apart of themselves," as it seemed, each time he touched them with the blade that itself was so blunt and bent over that the older man no longer deigned to use it himself.

He reckoned the boy to be approximately six feet tall and exactly six inches in height, including the expanse

that had opened up during the maturation process between his pantaloons and vest. But when it came time to
weigh the child, Lee could only guess at the number which
kept changing back and forth in his estimation from
around 260 pounds to as little as 240. It made Lee mad,
remembering his own size, which had never been like this.
And meantime the sticks were flying, the churl hewing,
and the blade singing in midair. Lee let several moments
go by before moving to a position whence he might better
view the creature's face.

It was a face of a certain kind and belonged to a person,
Lee would have said, who ought never have left his upland
home among inert volcanoes in the state's northeastern
part—such were his thoughts when, that moment, he
chanced to see Judy coming toward them with a platter of
what were probably beans, bread, and the usual honey.

He thought that he might faint. The vagrant had not
finished one part of the work that Lee had in store for
him, and here now was Judy again throwing away their
beans by hundreds upon any passing stranger with wit
enough to use a spoon.

"A meal like that? Judy, Judy. Why do you want to put
our guest under a moral obligation like that?"

The churl seemed not to hear. He had finished the
beans at once, had drunk the honey, and now was probing
with one finger into a corner of the plate where nothing
remained.

"Would you like some more?" Lee's wife asked before
Lee could catch hold of her.

"More! Can't you see he simply wants to be left alone?
So he can work?"

The scoundrel was of course supplied with further
beans, additional honey, and two full cups of high-cost
coffee. It was while Lee was counting up his losses that the
youth tried to rise and almost came crashing down on top

of them.

"He's tired!" said Judy. "Very tired. And he wants to lie down, too!"

Lee looked at her, she in her lipstick and the red sloppy ribbon in her hair. Soon they'd have no rations left at all, with policies such as hers. Nevertheless, Lee came forward and began nudging the boy (three-fourths asleep already) toward the barn.

Later on, thinking back upon it, he was to remember the fear that came down over the child when he set eyes for the first time on those book-lined precincts with its tables and desk, its two microscopes, hand crank computer, and the some twenty-odd framed engravings affixed to plywood walls where but until recently only mules had dwelled, living in unfurnished cells. Standing back, Lee, who had prepared this place many years ago in hopes of guests—no guests had come—examined the area with his all-too-critical eye.

"Yes," he said, addressing the boy from about twenty feet away, "no doubt it does seem like a great many books, for someone of your sort. And yet, compared to the house"—he nodded toward the house—"this is absolutely nothing, a mere residuum as it were, or 'reserves,' we call them, Judy and me, when compared, I say, with what you see yonder through that middle window with the . . ."

The knave wasn't listening. He had chosen the old-fashioned bedstead in the adjoining compartment, an inviting piece of equipment covered with a faded quilt showing scenes from the battles of John Bell Hood. Many times Lee had resorted to this bed when on winter nights he had craved to hear the language of the rain on a paper-thin roof. But instead of rain, and in lieu of Lee, the churl now lay sprawled at full length, overhanging the furniture in several places.

"Ah, me," said Lee, "if only *he'd* been there, there at Franklin with the others." (He pointed to the quilt, a bloody piece of work showing what had happened on a certain bad day in Tennessee.) "I believe we could have won."

"Ssssh! He's sleeping."

"But oh, my goodness, the ignorance. And look at that face!"

"Really, we ought to take off his shoes."

"'We?'"

"All right, I'll do it myself then!"

Lee caught her. There was not the slightest chance that he would permit her into the shoes of such a one as that, an outlander and hill dweller unclean and predominantly ignorant and so full of honey that Lee could not endure to think of what it had done to their supplies. He had little trouble, as short as his wife had lately become, in lifting her from the floor and, while she stood kicking and fuming, transporting her outdoors.

"No, dear, *I'll* be the one to cope with the shoes, yes? And you, why this will give you the time to go and prepare our own meal, yours and mine!"

No. She stood unsmilingly until at last Lee turned and tiptoed back to where the creature lay snoring among books and paraphernalia and, withal, the best accommodations this side of River Cahawba. Quickly he cut loose the moccasin on the boy's left-hand side and tossed it as far from himself as he could, where it bounced against the wall. No socks. Nor did the boy seem to require them. Suddenly Lee uttered out loud, dismayed to find that the remaining foot, the one in leather, was fitted with a prosthetic device of strange nature, crude beyond imagination, the work most likely of some fellow tribesman, an iron monger possibly, or good-intentioned smith who had wanted by such means to make the legs more or less equal in length by comparison to each other. Lee dropped it at once, but then immediately gathered it up again and fastened it back into place.

Of the boy's upper parts, his face for example and head in general, they belonged to a person of whom it was difficult to make final judgment. Next, working tenderly, Lee lifted the lid on the right-hand side, uncovering an eye that was large, hazel, and highly clarified. It was not uncommon to come across features of this kind, hazel ones, in certain upriver counties toward the north. Thinking on this (and taking out his pipe and filling it), he was slow to drop the lid and slow, too, in running around to the other side where the eye proved so much like the first one that right away Lee began to confuse them in his mind.

Outside, his wife was where he had placed her. "I'm thinking we should have the ham tonight," he said, "and black-eyed peas. You're very hungry and . . ."

"Is he all right?"

"Fine, fine. Knows how to sleep certainly! Yes, indeed." He hummed. "There *is* that little . . . how to say? Anomaly."

She stopped.

"No, no, no, *I* didn't do it. It's one leg, you see—shorter than the other. And that will explain his limp. For my part, I think we should have gravy with the ham and gravy with the grits."

She said nothing. Knowing her only too well, Lee was quick to point out that:

"He doesn't belong to us, dear. Why, he's nearly a full-grown man!"

"What's his name?"

"Never asked. And I will *not* have you plucking some adorable little name out of mid-air and foisting it off onto him like you did for . . ." (He mentioned here the dog, who also had come to them from out of the hills.) "Anyway, he'll be gone by tomorrow."

"Oh, don't be ridiculous. Who would feed him?"

It nearly always gave Lee pleasure when at the end of a tumultuous day he would throw himself inside the house and, shivering with the most delicious sense of security, pull Judy in after him.

He looked upon it as his own special place, and never mind that the structure was too tall by far and excessively narrow for its height. As to the *ceilings* (and the house was full of them), they were so high that only with great difficulty could he actually perceive them, and even then, he had to use his better glasses. But primarily it was the wallpaper he adored, hundred-year-old stuff so faded by now and so grainy that it turned one's thoughts to classic nineteenth-century postage stamps. Many were the times he used to stand facing that wall with his lantern, endeavoring to read those old newspaper accounts wherewith the paper had been mended and patched. But mostly he was drawn to the damp places where some of his earliest ancestors had been immured.

There were a number of things that committed him to this place and marked him out, not so much as "the captain of his own destination" as rather the captive, so to speak, of self-fascination. But all this was as nothing when held up next to the objects (books) and items (musical recordings) that he had abstracted from New York City, hundreds of good things that filled the shelves that ran back and forth and extended even unto the ceiling itself where a ladder was needed to get them down. They covered the moist places, the books did, and offered tens of thousands of pages amongst which a person could hide his bills of money.

He was aware of everything—the furniture, the mice, the smell of mildew, calomel, and soot. Aware, too, that the closet was full of canned foods. Climbing to the third floor, he also became aware of Judy who, often as not, would be seated on the floor among her belongings.

These were the good years. No one whom he had ever known had any desire to find him. In Africa, meantime, and points further east, sixteen wars were being carried out with sticks, rifles, and razor blades. One could do worse than pilot even such an unwieldy house as this one over the dark, deep, and unsettled sea that comprised a typical black night in the land called Alabama.

And: "Did I not say, dear," (he said), "that our love would persist for ten thousand years?"

She couldn't hear him, not so long as he remained in his vestibule, a narrow space beneath the stairs where he had room but for a chair, lamp, and old-fashioned radio that had gone bad except for certain highly irregular wave lengths in the extreme right-hand region of the dial. Approaching the thing with circumspection—it was as big, almost, as the refrigerator—he now switched on the motor and prepared himself for a very long wait. Thus, several minutes went by, which is to say until some of the more conspicuous tubes (the machine had long ago lost its housing and was kept together with rubber bands) until the essential tubes, as he was saying, began to blush and, finally, throw off sparks.

Somehow, he had tapped into a comedy show, an uproarious affair that had originated from somewhere in Chicago shortly before the War. Coming nearer, he did his best to understand the jokes but soon was overwhelmed by blasts of trash music breaking in from two neighboring channels. It was quite useless—each time he thought that he was at last keening in on the old songs, that was when postmodernity took possession of the wires.

Turning to the news, he heard two stories each about racism and price movements. Quickly he turned off the power, waited, counted and then, bending over the machine, tried to ascertain if the tubes had cooled sufficiently and whether he could find Chicago amid the static.

They ate in silence, the woman and Lee. Good years were these, now that the tedium of youth was behind them; they liked to sit for hours in the dim, gloating conjointly over what they had accomplished in the past and what they hoped to avoid in the future. And in short, he foresaw for them nothing but music and dogs, nights and long walks in the increasingly depopulated countryside. Suddenly, that moment, the radio spoke out loud and clear, Lee having forgotten to turn it off. And because it was a weather report (their favorite kind of listening), and since it referred to a nearby locality and to current time, Lee chose to give heed to it and, if possible, memorize it before too much static got between the meteorologist and he.

Thunder and rain, coming from opposite directions, were anticipated on two different fronts. And someday, he knew, great balls of fire would come rolling down the valley, evaporating the Cahawba. Bending nearer, he learned that December would be upon them much sooner than he had provided for. It promised high winds, the premier danger in these parts to his all-too-narrow and excessively tall home that already listed to one side.

"December," he said, looking meaningfully at his wife.

She paled. This was the weather that each year sent her running for her mittens and earmuffs and never mind that there were still 60 degrees of mercury both inside and out.

"But if you think *this* is chilly, just you wait till . . ."

"No, Lee, don't. Please."

". . . till snow has filled the attic, and little hills of frost sit athwart your nipples, *then* what will you do, hmm?"

She shivered violently and put on an anguished expression. Lee watched calmly as she tore loose the shawl that adorned the sofa and wrapped herself in it. The radio was continuing, a lugubrious voice telling of:

". . . high water in Tennessee."

"Tennessee!" said Lee. "Oh my, now that *is* getting close, isn't it?"

"How close is it, Lee?"

Not immediately answering, he began to do the mental geography in his head. These were the good years, and he foresaw no true danger for them, or anyway not for so long as they remained in a county that itself lay in the shade of a thousand defunct volcanoes, a peerless defense against all sorts of weather, northern invasions, interest rates, and television beams.

He had wanted to do the dishes; instead, at the last moment, a crime show came on, emanating from the only station he could trust. Of the story itself and its outcome, he was able to recall only very little of it later on. *His* preoccupation was with the way the world was when first the radio waves had set out on their long journey over the fields and furrows of Illinois. Meantime in the kitchen his wife was up to her elbows in dishes and, although he could decipher no word of it, singing non-stop.

He woke in time to find the radio clogged with noise, a bright moon outside, and Judy standing in front of him fitted out for bed. Fifty years and more she had been using the same suit of pajamas, a faded costume with a pattern of little bears on it, each bear dressed just like Judy.

"I'm ready," she said.

He came slowly to his feet and then, taking the precautions that he owed to his arthritis, lifted her in both arms. Tonight she had chosen to sleep on the third story where she kept the major portion of her opera recordings. And someday, he knew, he would grow too old to lift and carry her up so many stairs.

"Are we there?"

"Not yet, dear." She was short and getting shorter but remained extraordinarily heavy for her age and weight. Finally, arriving at her pallet, he lowered her carefully and, turning her, began kneading her along the connective tissue—she fell asleep at once—among her shoulders and spine.

"Are you going to be up all night, Lee?"

"Probably."

"Thinking about all the things you hate?"

He nodded. One would have thought she was still conscious, to judge by how she continued watching through the imperfect roof for what admittedly was an unduly bright moon.

"Lee?"

"Yes?"

"I'm ready to go to sleep now."

Lee said nothing. "You are asleep, dear."

She smiled radiantly, pleased to hear it. Having delayed as long as he could, he now came down, gathered the dog, again climbed the stairs, and planted the animal, still suffering from bad dreams, at the foot of Judy's rather untidy arrangement. Finally, as the last of his duties, he went around to each door and tested every latch, making absolutely certain that the little hooks comported rightly with their accompanying eyelets.

These hours were best when, with his books and tobacco, his three newspapers (one from France) and, of course, the radio, he would make up a place for himself in some unguessable part of the house where trespassers would least likely be able to find him. Here, chuckling to himself, he might spend a full hour dithering with the radio, or thinking thoughts, or, reverting again to the radio, narrowing in upon inadvertent voices coming from Montevideo and places even further than that. Or, he might doze off for a moment or two, good experiences during which his over-encumbered mind was vouchsafed a period of much-appreciated sleep. Refreshed by that, he might then return to his newspaper and, calling upon his Will to keep the pages lined up properly (one with another), proceed direct to the obituaries to see if he could find inscribed there the names of those—(and they were thousands)—who had wronged him in the past. Next, he resorted to the comic section, still looking for certain old-time favorite characters of his, most of them defunct by now. Finding nothing, he turned again to the radio and, holding it together in both hands, pressed it ever more tightly to his ear.

These then were his activities when, toward two, he fell into a medium-grade sleep that was constantly and perhaps even deliberately interrupted by last summer's last surviving cricket, the most malicious being ever to have found a way into Leland's home. He knew better than to rise, light the lantern, and go searching for the thing. Instead, he sought about for the newspaper (mankind's sloppiest invention), and after squandering forty-five seconds trying to align the pages and then another thirty going to fetch his stapler, turned back to the four-day-old weather forecast that showed again what awful prophets were those who spent their lives making predictions about the climate and the sky—never yet had he known a single one of them to apologize for anything. They were not perfect, these people, whereas the editorialists were *far* from perfect. But farthest of all were the obituaries, a half-page of highly partial accounts that shied away from details and gave no hint of the iniquities that some of these people, certainly, had carried out while still in health.

He read two editorials and remained of two minds as to whether both had been authored by the same nincompoop. Nor was the radio very much better. No matter where he turned, a deep-voiced man kept breaking in with the Spanish language. Finally, Lee gave it up and went to retrieve his copy of Herodotus, a two-volume translation in which the illustrator had shown how it must have looked on that day when the holy Grecian soil had been heaped three and four deep with slaughtered Medes. He stared at it with satisfaction and then, so as not to gorge himself on details, took another nap.

Moon of Alabama! it was ever dodging in and out, sometimes taking up unexpected positions in the sky. Lee, too, had to change positions several times if he wanted to go on reading by its beams. Far away, down in the valley and miles outside of town, he heard coyotes summoning all the world's dogs to come and join them. Very glad was he to be inside at this time and lodged in a building with adequate supplies, two rifles, much ammunition, and troves of books that had been broken down into more or less discrete collections and apportioned among the rooms. Reveling over it, he began to hum, and humming saw something then that *almost made him faint.*

Perhaps he screamed as well, and screaming jumped up and ran to the kitchen where the nearest large knives were kept. Of his pistol, he had left that in the truck where he could by no means get at it without exposing himself to the person whose immense shadow blocked the window and shut off all view of the moon.

"No!" he yelled. "Back, I say, go back to your barn!"

After an experience like that he had to force himself to return to his mattress, shut down the radio, and take up the newspaper. Impossible to go on reading in the quasi-light; indeed, he was doing well to make out even the largest fonts. New troubles, he read, had been uncovered in the neighboring county, eventuating in a scandal that filled the greater portion of the page. Lifting his glasses, he examined the photograph of the man described by the writer as the guiltiest of them all. Lee, however, doubted it. He had seen *far* worse than that, thousands of them riding off to work on subway cars. No, he would have said the person was but a standard criminal of the public kind, a favorite of the people. No, it was the *other* one, the man in the background who worried Lee.

Three o'clock had come and nearly gone before he grew aware of Judy wandering at large throughout the house. He waited for her, listening to the sound of her steps coming sometimes nearer and sometimes further as she searched among his wonted locations.

"Lee, Lee!"

"I'm here."

"It's so *quiet*, Lee, and it doesn't seem right. I woke and it was so *quiet*."

"No, no, it's always like this when the furnace is cold, and the dog has quit dreaming."

"Oh."

"And then, too, there's no traffic down along the highway at this hour." (He spoke rapidly, hoping she would not notice the monster standing at the window.) "And so, I recommend you just pad on back to bed and . . ."

"Sleep?"

"Exactly."

And did so. He watched as she moved away, dragging behind her the longest and at the same time the most mellow pillow in the house. Would she, or would she not, disregard his suggestion and put on an opera recording at this untoward hour?

He woke once more during that by-now famous night, coming awake to the sound of riotous music from the attic. He could not but smile, saying:

"It's only Judy, Judy and her music, Judy at 4:18 in the morning. No doubt she will have unwrapped her new album and will be listening to it up there—an old-world opera recording, unless I miss my guess." And saying so, he turned and rolled and was on the verge of napping again when he began to pick up faint strains of a very different music coming from the basement.

"It's only an anomaly of some kind," said he to himself, "or else she's trying two new albums at once." (Or maybe he had been granted his wish at last—the house was big enough—and now he had two Judies instead of just one.) "Me, I'm going back to sleep again."

He could not, however, Lee, go back to sleep again. Instead, after tallying up the hours he actually had slept and writing it down, he rose and tiptoed to the kitchen and satisfied himself that in this one room at least everything was as it should be. And yet, somehow, he knew that something was askew.

It was, of course, the churl—he was gone, missing, and the window where but until recently he had been positioned, there was nothing in it. Lee also had been wrong about the sun, which had arisen while he was thinking of other things. It was larger than Europe, theatrical beyond belief. He could not glare back at it without blinking. At once he retreated into the next room and, finding a pencil, jotted down the precise time of its arrival, intending to compare it against what the newspaper had predicted. Outside, meantime, the boy was tossing up lengths of wood and breaking them apart in mid-air.

Two

Atop the weathervane perched the rooster in great pride. Lee continued on to the barn where he knocked twice politely and, smiling, stepped inside. He noticed right away that the boy *had* tried to make the bed, even if he lacked the science of it. As to his possessions, a wool cap with a bill on it and a flute of some sort fashioned out of bamboo, he had placed these carefully one on top of the other and appeared ready now to take his departure.

"I can always tell," said Lee, "when someone has been interfering with my books."

The monster blushed horribly, started to speak, but then instead took up his cap and began running it through his hand.

"Yes, I would have seen that something was wrong even if you had returned the book precisely to where it's supposed to be. But of course, you didn't, did you?"

He thought for a moment the boy might actually cry.

"And what's the story with that leg of yours? That 'brace,' if that's what it is, it's no good. We both know that."

He simply would not let Lee look into his face.

"And that hair! Great God, how long ever has it been since last anyone trimmed it, eh? That's right, put your little cap back on so nobody can see it. Lord, Lord. Have you had breakfast? No, I didn't think so."

Someday, he knew, the time must come when they'd have no honey left at all; now, lifting the waffles on his spatula, he transported them one by one to the barn until the batter ran dry.

"Yes, she fixes a good pancake, the woman does. And while you're feeding, I think I'll just take a little peek at the book that you chose to . . ."

He jumped back, surprised at the quality of the thing. Indeed, it was one of Lee's favorites among those that he had deemed not quite precious enough to store inside the house.

"Thumbprint," he said, pointing to the smudge the boy had left on the title page. "Well you've done it now— ruined it."

He regretted it at once, a comment like that. The boy turned and gazed at him with eyes so sad and hollow that it reminded Lee of the people of the last century, who always looked so miserable when confronted by someone with a camera.

"How old are you boy?"

He did not know his own age, as Lee could see by the way he continued to wring out his cap, sometimes hiding it completely in the cavity of his enormous hand.

"I hope he's not getting mad at me," said Lee to himself. "A hand like that. Moses!"

He never enjoyed reading out loud, Lee did not, and yet, after three pages and with the emotion getting the better of him, he saw that he would have to go on with it until he came to a stopping place. Far away, through the window and across the yard, he saw Judy emerge from the house with her basket and go trundling forward in her hen-like gait toward where the hens themselves dwelled in a tumble-down shack in need of paint. Next, she would be peeping in upon the bees, who in recent days had transferred their nest to a hollow pumpkin shell. Lee, however, kept on reading, arriving finally at that part where the Greeks, hideously outnumbered, had come to a hilltop whence they could descry any number of little oared ships riding hopefully in the roads of the amethyst sea. Here Lee stopped, unwilling to let the boy see the moisture in his eyes.

A moment of silence followed. The churl, moaning softly, had begun rocking back and forth between the cot and the desk that supported Leland's hourglass.

"Do you read, boy? English prose? No, no, it's all right, just go ahead and take it," he said, preferring to hand the book over to him than to go on reading out loud.

He opened it tenderly, the boy did, and drew the thing up close to his face. Lee watched as he lifted the page, a thin item printed on both sides, and laid it to rest. Who was it had sent this boy here, and why did that person imagine that Lee did not already have enough to do?

"But can you *read*, boy? R-E-A-D? No, probably not— he's returning the book to its place and seems to be choosing another."

He had selected his book, had the monster, a blue one in cloth covers. Now, turning his back upon Lee, he began either to read or at any rate to run his eyes across the material. Lee let twenty seconds go by, till curiosity brought him to the boy's side.

"Please don't use your finger like that," he said. "It gets in the way, and I can't see." (That was when he realized the finger had stopped at a certain word, a four-syllable affair that, really, the child could not be expected to understand.) "Ah!" said Lee to himself. "He begins to see how ignorant he is." And then, speaking out loud: "You begin to see how ignorant you are?"

The boy nodded.

"We saw it right away, the wife and me. And now you want me to fix it, don't you? Lord, Lord. As if I didn't have enough already. House needs painting, and so forth." (He looked at the boy meaningfully, until at last the solution seemed to register on him.) "But will the ladder hold you?"

"No Lee, he can't do anything if he doesn't have any clothes." (Apparently his wife had come into the room at some point and had been listening to the recitation.)

"Certainly, he has clothes!"

"Oh, I suppose. But they aren't any good."

That was true. Lee went and lifted the boy's trouser leg, exposing again the corrective device that had been fastened to him on that side. As to how he had limped so far, traveling overland against the grain of northern Alabama—it was a mystery.

By early afternoon the child's head had been shorn and the hair itself carted out into the field and burned. Dressed now in a bright yellow blouse that had belong to one of Leland's forebears, he sat quietly, waiting for his host to pick up reading again.

"We have seen what happened to the Greeks," said Lee, "and now this afternoon we'll focus on other things, or at least until my throat goes dry." (The book was small enough and fitted perfectly into the pocket of his vest.

Drawing it out as if it were a gun, Lee threw it open and began reading in dark voice about a sequence of wars that had brought so much bale into the then-known world. Ten minutes of this, with the wars growing more and more awful and the child moaning and swaying, Lee's voice began to taper down to a mere whisper in which, however, the emotion still managed to communicate it-self. Finally, having worked his way to the end of the chapter, he stopped, snapped shut the book, and smiled at both his listeners.

Later on, thinking back on it, he was not willing to say that his guest had actually made threats or anything of that sort. And yet, such was his behavior that Lee did not feel free to discontinue reading at that time. Moving hur-riedly to the next chapter, he smiled and read three pages more before his voice grew completely invisible and he was reduced to using hand signals, as inadequate as these were. "Certainly, he must loathe me a very great deal," said Lee to himself, "the one who sent him here. Will he *never* leave? And those hazel eyes!"

Insofar as he could, Lee went on reading therefore, nonplused to find that each time he glanced up the child had positioned himself at a different remove. It was not until Lee caught him sitting in the loft with his legs dan-gling over the edge that he dared finally to rise and throw himself and his wife outside and run across to the house.

Three

He woke a little earlier than usual, rose, and moved around the room. The woman was spending the night in the basement, to judge from the direction of the music. Finally, Lee summoned enough courage to turn the televi-sion on, but then immediately shut it off again as soon as he had verified the subject matter.

The moon was not much better; examining it both
with and without his glasses, he succeeded at last in plac-
ing himself up to his knees in imagination upon that
yielding surface where he could not make a move without
streams of powder pouring in over the tops of his boots.
Coming back to earth, he noticed a light burning in the
barn.

"He has learned to use the lantern," said Lee, pleased
by the churl's progress but also worried that he might
burn the building down. "Sitting on the edge of the bed, I
ween, groaning away the night!" It inspired him to go in
search of his telescope, a child's instrument that, however,
served well enough over short distances. Aiming first at
the moon—the rotten spots were expanding—he focused
next upon the boy, or upon his neck and shoulders rather,
which blocked off any view of what he might be reading.
Lee was surprised. He had such a fragile way, the boy did,
with the pages, lifting and lowering the things one by one
and then very often going back to give a second and even
a third inspection to earlier matter.

Lee yelled at him, yelling in vain. The moon had
dropped below the horizon and apparently had exploded,
liberating whole coveys of woe-betiding crows. Returning
to his French newspaper, Lee now also began to read,
reading of the deterioration that seemed always to be going forward in that country. But was not this that same
nation where so many famous kings had once held sway,
intimidating with Power the foolish population? He regretted them, Lee did, those kings, a sagacious people who
had known just the moment to climb down off the throne
and file away before modernity had well set in.

Probably he slept. And when next he grew aware of
himself, the music was gone, the moon was down, and the
dog (who had come all the way from the third story), was
studying him closely from two inches away. Lee, never

blinking, used his Will upon the creature, forcing him back with the more powerful of his two eyes.

It was that same eye he used for the telescope; now, crowding at the window, he verified that the boy was still in place, still reading, still lifting gingerly the pages and letting them down, still fascinated, as it seemed, by their resemblances to each other and their surpassing thinness.

He dressed slowly, Lee, went outside and had tiptoed halfway across the yard before admitting that he had come away without shoes. Returning for them, he then approached the barn obliquely and took up a post just outside the window. Very soon the boy would also need glasses, if he continued to do his reading in such feeble light. And then, too, a cloud of gnats and other nuisances had gathered around the lantern. Next, taking his spyglass and adjusting it finely, Lee saw at last which book it was the child was reading. Satisfied, he might almost have gone back and grabbed off a few more hours of sleep, had not the vagrant chosen that moment to close the book and push it off to one side.

"Hey!" called Lee, rapping at the same time on the glass. "You haven't read *half* that book, for pity's sake!"

The boy gathered it up at once and, blushing deeply, opened it again, even if not at the precise place where he had left off. Lee waited for his anger to subside somewhat before going around to the entrance and stepping inside.

"Goddamn it, you're going to need that book boy, yes and ten-thousand others if you expect to turn the world upside down." (He sank down in the chair, the only one the room afforded. Looking into the child's face, he could detect no obvious lessening of ignorance there in spite of his reading.)

"Ten thousand books," Lee went on, "and at least one modern European language. You'll need to know about guns, of course, and how to speak in front of large groups. Me, I can't do it; I'm too old. What, am I going too fast?"

The boy was writing it down with a pen that Lee had never seen before, a capacious instrument, grand enough to hold a pint of ink. Bending nearer, the older man was astonished both by his speed and by the script itself that seemed so small and typographic in comparison with the hand that formed it. To encourage him, Lee said:

"Why, he writes rather well, he really does. Wonder where he acquired *that?*" And then after a pause: "Where'd you learn that, son?"

But instead of replying, the child cocked his head to one side, as if engrossed in Judy's music coming from the house.

"Like Puccini do you?"

The knave nodded, but whether he was being honest Lee could not with certainty say. And yet there did seem to be some little mist and smoke in that part of the face that could not altogether be hidden from Leland's gaze.

"Better for you if you left here at once. Do you hear?"

He *seemed* to hear. Thinking back on it, Lee would have said the boy was especially susceptible just then, an empty weapon, as it were, that might be filled with any sort of ammunition.

"But if you stay . . . Oh! Why then you must study wisdom in that case—I'll show you how—and acquire the means to turn the world about."

There was nothing in his face to show that he was surprised by these suggestions. Lee counted up to six, saying:

"It appears you're still here. You'll be sorry for that."

From the house, the opera had reached its high part. Taking advantage of it, the older man now planted himself behind the boy and began whispering to his left ear, telling strange things that had to do with books and music and the molten hatreds of which Lee had so many. Watching from her window, the woman (who had no hatreds of her own), must have thought it was the smiling Devil himself pouring libels into that fallow ear.

Four

It rained that night again. Pressing at the window, he witnessed four successive lightning strikes, jagged and bright, aimed apparently at the city that lay half-a-mile below them in the valley. And yet these, too, failed to give him much pleasure, knowing, as he did, how trivial the damage might be as compared to what was needed. He tried the radio, finding naught but static. Some static, of course, was better than none, and in one place he came upon what might have been a secret message code. But nothing worried him more than this, namely that the house was too tall for its width and someday in bad weather the whole system might topple off into the valley.

He found his wife at the bottom of the building, happy in her apron. He did so love it, to come upon her unawares and catch her talking to herself with congruent facial expressions. Oh yes, he *could* have pounced upon her, for what that might be worth, and been rewarded with a scream, a hobby of his that he indulged less and less often as the condition of her heart deteriorated and her screams grew weaker. No, these days he preferred to follow her secretly about the house and then astonish her later on with a full report about everything that she had done.

But not tonight. He was tired, and the churl was nervous. Using the telescope, he saw that the boy was reading for but short spells only, and then rising and limping back and forth within his narrow quarters. A book lay open on the table, but with his amateurish telescope Lee could not actually read the print. There was also a tidy pile of note paper covered in the boy's uncanny script ("runes," Lee called them), together with a satirical drawing of an older man wearing dense glasses and carrying a tiny telescope in one hand.

"We're talking about his *whole* life," said Lee, speaking to the empty room, "and whether or not he's willing to

pick up where the Greeks and I left off. I must be patient."
His words were followed by a thunderclap, a good sign,
Lee believed, that boded enormous benefits for later on.

Lee logged two hours at his desk, until at last his mind
began to clear and he was able to dip his pen and fill it, as
it were, in his own intellectual sediment that tonight was
richer and somewhat more friable than usual. Starting of
course with the Greeks, he then jotted down a whole
schedule of titles that veered rather toward Byzantium
instead of Rome. Having filled the sheet with essential
titles, he came to a sudden stop at the seventh century
where he could think of nothing worth mentioning. Bending low over the list—(anyone seeing him would have
thought he was sleeping)—he inspected the paper at close
range, examining its pores and fibers, and the very fanciful
watermark that put him in mind of the iconography of
Persia's royal house. This ennui often came over him
when he was working in weak light upon the sixth, seventh, and, very frequently, the eighth and even later cen-
turies. Led astray by it, he realized too late that he had
skipped forward to Jagiellonian affairs, a time and a place
that had nothing whatsoever to do with the boy and his
education. "Ah, me," he said, "I am thinking of several
things at once, and my list is getting out of order." And
saying so, he forced his mind forward a few hundred years
where the titles began to come "of themselves," as it were,
if not indeed even more rampantly than he wanted. Thus
Lee who, after ten minutes of this exercise, rose and went
to the window and after checking on the boy, came back
and turned on the radio.

He had expected to find Chicago on the dial; instead he
had broken in upon a small town in Oklahoma that required him to take down the atlas and use his best glasses
in order to locate it in the extreme southwestern region of
that state. An important highway entered that town but

never came out again, if one could trust the mapmaker. Lee marked its position on the radio dial, consigning Chicago itself and everything in it to a sort of mental limbo where he expected never to hear from it again. One could do worse than give one's attention to a small town with a low-watt station on the other side of the horizon.

Now once again his own mind was highly divided, some of it thinking about Oklahoma, some about thunder, and some about the list of books he was compiling for the thrall. No works in Greek or Latin! There simply wasn't time for it. That was when it occurred to him to interlard certain select pieces of music into the list, that the boy might listen to them when he grew tired of reading.

3:45 found him on the toilet with the Cambridge Medieval History in his lap. Among other things, he had chosen several of the greater hermit authors for the boy to read, "desert fathers," so-called, stalactite sitters and others of that kind, weird people who, they too, had sought to turn the world around.

Far away he heard an airplane driving by, a reminder of the century in which he was actually living. "*Another* airplane," he said darkly, "and with a cargo full of people who had rather go places than read about them." He could feel his gorge rising. Shutting both eyes and squeezing them tight, he next tried to steer the plane by force of Will alone and bring it down among the thunder clouds.

He made three more trips to his bookshelves, returning at last to the toilet with volume number two of Burton's *Melancholy*, the most plenteous source that he had so far found for titles that in these days were the most often ignored. Smacking his lips over it, he began transcribing hastily, adding to Reuben's list. Came also to mind the names of four modern philosophers notorious for their ideas.

Thus Lee—stationed as he was in his high place with his legs dangling down, he toiled on manfully and with humility until five o'clock in the morning, a testimony to his faith in the boy. But when toward dawn he began to hear crows congregating outside, the sound of traffic along the highway, and music from the upper stories, at that time he arose and put a stop to list making and after then wasting several minutes in what was almost certainly a vain effort to preordain his dreams, went to sleep.

Sometimes he would sleep a full six or seven hours out of the twenty-four, doing it in discrete quanta of unlike length. Tonight, he dreamt that he was hiding behind a wall while below him in the valley a horde of northern progressives was trying to muster the courage to come and find him. But in lieu of any sort of effective weapon, he found that he had been given an old-fashioned musket that had seen too much service and in any case was capable of releasing but one ball at a time. Nevertheless, even so, he was ready to "play the cards that had been dealt him," his favorite platitude. Now, taking off his glasses, he brought the musket up to his best eye and drew a bead upon a tall lanky fellow, a New York man, judging by his smirk and value system. Lee fired once, and once was all he needed; right away the scum fell to his knees and then pitched forward to kiss with shredded lips the southern earth.

"Hee!" he called. (He was thinking of what he could have done with a modernistic gun.) "Hee, hee!" Turning his aim next upon a portly man, Lee simply shot him where he sat. "Right in the belly!" He could have spent years in this activity, could Lee, going without food, rest, books, or any of it. For loving history, but hating how it had turned out, he saw it as a chance to turn the course of events around. That was when his wife came and brought him back to his own times.

"Lee, no, it's all right baby. Here, drink this."

He obeyed.

"Oh, Lee. Was it the ecstasy again? Someday you're going to hurt yourself."

He finished the drink, hot vodka with cinnamon in it. Day had dawned, such as it was, and stood in sullen array at the window, a sight more repellent than the foregoing black night. "This will be the day," he said, "when Western civilization comes to an end. I always knew it would look like this." And saying so, he went to fill the cup again, pausing only to fetch down his copy of Denniston's delectable *Greek Particles*, the only kind of reading for weather like this.

By ten o'clock, he had taken his cot outside and was hoping with the aid of this morning's grainy light to grab off another hour's worth of medium-grade sleep. The rain was gone and the thunder, too, and soon he found himself in an eye contest with the sun running like a wheel over uneven ground. Changing glasses, he espied two pale morning stars being sucked ever so helplessly—it gave him a panicky feeling—into the sun's superior mass. Day *had* come, he knew it from the evidence that was all around him. But where now, pray, were the golden squashes of last summer that he had sowed with his own two hands amongst roses and marjoram? Gone, all gone, gone with the scuppernongs and gone with the plums.

Eventually he arose and, still carrying his bed with him, took up a position on the brow of the hill. In languor here, he was prepared for the cries and shrieks of the city that lay half-a-mile beneath him, an amalgamated noise in which he could sometimes pick out individual voices that had become well-known to him over the course of years.

So. Mild day it was, compared to what January would likely bring. He liked to lie on his belly and alternate his attention between the book and the gigantic sculpture that had been set up in the valley in remembrance of his favorite philosopher, a mustachioed man shown gazing up with bulging eyes at thoughts too horrible for ordinary people to consider. (He knew of course that it was only the statue of a basketball player, and that great concrete orb that ought have represented the world, that in fact it was the ball.) Rather than to continue looking at such things, he again took up his bed and went sixty yards with it before settling beneath . . .

. . . a waterfall (he called it) of grey Spanish Moss. "Ah, me," he said. His wife meantime had come outside and was traveling in her duck-like gait toward the henhouse to see if things were right with them. No! No, she had changed course at the last moment and was moving instead toward the hogs. Lee chuckled and then, turning to the reader, said: "She does so love it, Judy does, to feed those creatures and watch the pleasure registering in their faces!" Again, he yawned and stretched and rolled over to allow the sun to warm his nether side. "Well, I reckon it's about time to let the churl out of the barn."

The "churl" in fact was waiting just inside the door, very anxious to go out into the field to relieve himself. In his absence, Lee was able to look at his work and go through the notebook full of drawings, not all of them bad. It seemed, too, as if someone had been using the computer. Lee had just time enough to clear away the four books that had not been properly returned to the shelf before the monster was back.

"Monkeying with my computer!" said Lee. "Very well. But just remember this, that no one ever attained *real* power by fooling around with binary things. Oh no, you'll have to do much better than that if you expect to take history in your teeth and turn the world about."

The boy looked at him, struggling to understand.

"Either seek power absolute, or else have nothing to do with people. Repeat it."

He did (repeat it), uttering the words slowly and with an expression of trouble on his half-hidden face. Lee observed how his left hand, a most impressive piece of equipment indeed, continued to open and close, as if in times to come it might really be grand enough to enclose the earth.

"Yes," said Lee, "there's no real choice for you, is there? *I'm* the one that has nothing to do with people."

He looked, the boy did, as if he wanted to cry. Far away, beyond the window and across the yard, Lee saw Judy come from the hog house and then, after casting a rueful look in his direction, go trundling toward the hives. A full half hour now must pass before either the man or monster would receive from her his meed of honey and waffles.

"She's a good woman, yes," said Lee. "Divine, in fact. But don't you start imagining that *you'll* ever have anything like that, not since women have opted to be like men. No, your job is to look upon women as . . ." He thought deeply, finally coming out with: ". . . a staircase to power."

The boy moved off into a corner of the room where Lee could not always see what he was thinking. The sun that only two hours ago had shouldered its way above the hills, already it was dropping behind, or rather into, one of the hollow volcanoes. All his life Lee had wanted to live in a place when, and a time where, daylight endured for just two hours or fewer.

"Hmm," he said, "getting dark! And Judy is two hundred yards from home. What do you plan on reading tonight?" But instead of allowing the varlet to answer, Lee suddenly plucked from his vest the schedule he had prepared, nineteen sheets of coarse-grained paper in which the ink had shifted over during the time of composition from a hue of royal blue all the way to glossy black. "Your itinerary," he said, spreading the pages on the floor. "And never mind that I had to stay up *all day* to get it done."

Both men now got down and, using the lantern, began to go over the list. Lee was pleased with the child's seriousness as one by one he lifted the pages, looked them over, and put them back. It was page number seven that held the real "cream," so to speak, thirty titles that meandered in and out of Classical literature before ending up with Nietzsche. Lee bent down low, hoping to see the boy's reaction.

"Don't you turn away from me like that, boy, when I'm trying to read that face!" And then in somewhat gentler tones: "Yes, it's hard to go through so many books in just a month or so. But remember this, that it's *supposed* to be hard. Otherwise we'd have all sorts of trash running around, their heads full of stuff. Well? Will you do it?"

The boy groaned. Lee could see how he kept coming back to page number four.

"And the sooner you do it, why then the sooner you can go!"

He smiled, the first such expression that Lee had ever seen in him.

"Yes! Leave and go away—*I* won't stop you. And how could I after all, an old man like me scarce able to bench press his own weight? And the woman, certainly *she* can't stop you. But first you must finish the list."

Again, the creature scooped up the sheets, fuddled with them, and then dealt them down flat (though not in perfect order) on the table and bed. He had fixed his attention on the first item of all, an action that satisfied the older man.

"Just look at that—he has targeted the first item of all. I'm pleased. It's a brief thing really, that book, and you should be finished with it by, oh, half past eleven?"

The child glared at him, Lee glaring back. Thus, passed full ten seconds before it came down on Lee with a burst of delight that the miscreant wanted to get started . . .

Now!

Five

Two days went by, or possibly three, a hazy period during which Lee kept resolutely to the house. He could not say for certain whether it were fog or whether smoke that filled the valley and ran into the mountains to join with clouds. And in short, it was a perfect time for reading about Anglo-Saxon England, when great mists used to come rolling in off the ocean and cover the people in a grey colloidal murk. These were the good days, when he would lie upon the floor and soak for hours in the finest music of all, Wagner and/or Mahler's.

Nothing angered him more than for the music to come to an end. And then, too, he maintained another grudge against that man (Wagner) for having died fifty years too soon. "Thank God for old history books!" he said, adding: "And Gustav Mahler. But wait, is that *Judy* over there standing in the dark? Yes, I believe it is!"

"It's coming under the door now, Lee."

"Fog?"

She nodded sadly.

"I see. Well, we could put on *Tristan* I suppose."

Two days more went by, a time of smoke and roses, lovely beyond belief. Many times, he went to check on Judy, each time to finish up by lying on top of her or sleeping within her arms. He liked to believe the world was over and nothing lay outside their door but fields and hills and extinct cities from which all the corpses had been removed. Or that their tall and, yes, ungainly house had floated away on the music to a time when people were few and far apart, and great fogs would come each day and stay a little longer.

"But Lee, we have lots of fog *tonight*."

"Yes! *That's* what I want," he said, adding with some bitterness: "Nobody likes it more than me, and nobody gets less of it." Suddenly he turned and looked at her, verifying that she hadn't changed in any important way since the last time he had seen her. That it was the same Judy and not some mere facsimile, he knew it from a thousand indications and her eyes. "Judy?"

"Yes?"

"Let's go away, you want to? Me and you?"

"All right."

"Some place where it's foggy and the people . . ."

"Are few and far apart?"

"Right!"

"That would be good. Or, we could just stay here."

There was a good deal of sense in what she said. The house they lived in, it would endure, he believed, for ten seasons more at least.

"And did I not say, dear, that our love would persist for ten thousand years?"

She thought about it. "You did, yes. Last year you said it. And the house, how long . . . ?"

"Ten."

She shivered at the thought of it, of going nine thousand years and more without a shelter of their own. "And then what, Lee?"

"Well! Then we turn into two vast mountains standing side by side throughout eternity." (He pointed to the volcano field.)

It seemed to satisfy her. The house had *not* drifted away, as he verified by going to the window. The barn, too, was intact, little spumes of smoke lifting from the stack. It caused him to believe that the creature was in place and working conscientiously on his future. Imagine then the old man's surprise when he found the child glued to the window again, his eyes squeezed tight as he harkened to Judy's opera with both ears pressed against the glass.

In spite of it, Lee was pleased. Using hand signals, he was able, first, to send the boy back to the barn and then, secondly, remind him of the items on his list.

The next hour Lee spent huddled in the corner, a protected sort of place where he could not be seen from any of the windows. His book was dense but good; he read two full chapters with profit and pleasure, until the outlandish nature of all those Cornish names and provinces began to confuse his head. It is true that he had been taking small quantities of liquor to fend off the cold. Finally, with the sun having come back for another of its brief stays, he rose up and went to collect his knife, a foot-long appliance stolen many years ago from a certain pawnshop in Pennsylvania.

He proceeded to oil the blade, an enjoyable work. He liked to lift the weapon on high and then come down with it, slicing through the atmosphere. Finally, having put a sheen on it, he wiped the perspiration from the blade and then suddenly lunged forward with it, a mad sort of behavior that ended up with both the knife and Lee facing approximately toward New York City.

At 3:15 Lee returned to the barn to find the churl was reading. On the desk, Lee spied two books, good ones— (*all* of Lee's books were good)—good ones lying in such a way as to hold open a third one that was itself both heavier and better than anything the runt had so far attempted up until this time.

"Goodness, you *are* making progress. And how many books have you read since Thursday?"

The boy counted. His hand, which was huge and which he used for a calculating machine, was still too slow and rustic-looking and the fingers still too blunt for the kind of digits that Lee expected in students of *his*.

"Nine, you say, nine since Thursday. No, I would have thought it twice that number at least. And just look at that, the disorder in those shelves!"

The boy blushed and turned away his face. Lee next inspected his daybook, finding it full of a penmanship that seemed actually to have deteriorated over the last days—which is to say until he got into his more comfortable glasses and then, bending near, jumped back suddenly when he saw that the varmint had been toying about with the first ten letters of the Attic alphabet.

They went out into the field, the older man lagging far behind. It gave Lee the chance to compare his own shadow against the boy's, an unflattering contrast that announced to him that he was getting old. He had spent the first four-fifths of his life thinking of himself as a young man, and now here on the ground was the evidence that his shade looked like a buzzard's as it trailed behind the one that looked like the boy's.

Some years prior to this Lee had invested in a dozen bales of hay; now, largely rotten, they remained there still, "men" of straw who fulfilled no other purpose than to frighten his wife when on clear nights she chanced to peep through the curtains. Toward the nearest of these large bales Lee and the boy now directed themselves. "Ah, me," said Lee, "the condition of this one is particularly poor. And someday, when it is rotten through and through, that will be when I am rotten, too. You noticed my shade?"

The bale stood taller than either of them. Taking the knife, Lee held it this way and that, until it caught up the late summer light in flecks along the shaft. "Take my knife," said Lee, feeling that he was handing over the last of his onetime youth. "Yes, and take my books and take my hatreds, too."

And did so, the boy did, accepting the weapon by the bone handle that bore an inlay of a Bavarian forest scene. Nor did Lee fail to note how those fingers of his traveled two times around the handle before coming back to the starting point. Dangerous beyond imagination and with eyes of grey, Lee moved back twenty paces, until out of range of the boy's utmost reach. From that position, Lee called out his instructions in a voice still hoarse from last week's readings.

"Imagine," he yelled, "that this straw person stands in lieu of what we both abhor. Continuing on, imagine that knife of yours is long enough to penetrate, not just persons merely, but schools of thought. Imagine further . . ." He stopped. All this talk about hatred and so forth was bringing back his headache, a thudding sensation that had begun to work its way through the conduits of his gorge.

"Take my youth," said Lee, "and take my books. Take my knowledge, and take my hate."

The boy nodded. He held the knife, Lee noted, like a harpoon.

"Take my knife," said Lee one more time, "and drive it up to the hilt in that philosophy there, the one that stopped our country from becoming like Greece."

And did so, a swift movement that damaged the hay at the level of the "man's" chest. Lee broke into tumultuous cheers that winged across the field, smote the silo, and bounced right back. He was good at it, the vagrant, and no one had ever been better with a knife.

"Stick it in his belly and make a lateral cut. Good."

Again, the boy lunged forward, an angular blow that served to cut away the fellow's nose.

"Lower and low, wicked and bad, veritably a nation of voters and sports fans. Put it in his ear and draw the blade down."

And did so, a powerful blow that made the meadows shake. It allowed Lee to see that a nest of mice had set up in the place where a heart should be.

"Don't forget the neck."

He did not, in the event, forget it. On the contrary, he laid it open with one fine stroke that exposed all the tendons there.

"Jove! And someday, Reuben, when you come to full powers . . . Ah child, it *will* be thee, or someone very like it, who in times to come will do what must be done—I *know* it!"

Far away, both men could hear new activity from the horizon where thunder was breaking apart the dilapidated clouds. Although still early in the afternoon, already night was bearing down upon them and the sun, such as it was, was dissolving even as they looked upon it. But as for *Judy* meantime, all that she could ever see were three gaunt people dancing madly on the heath.

Six

He was gloating about being asleep and unconscious when, suddenly, he heard his wife calling up to him.

"Lee! Lee!"

He arose at once.

"Lee, Lee, winter's coming in!"

Two stories below him in the yard, she looked like a dot jumping up and down. Lee, who agreed about the season, smiled and thanked her for it. Further in the distance he could see Reuben trundling through the weeds with his net, chloroform, magnifying glass, and the other paraphernalia needed for his course of studies (designed by Judy) on insect speciation in the field. Further still, *too* far really, he could make out his great-grandfather's immensely tall memorial tower that bent back and forth like

a whip in the wind and marked the Edge of the world in
that direction.

"How, I say how do you know that winter's coming in?"

"Because!"

She was right. The dog was racing in a circle around
the churl, while nearer to home the hens seemed nervous.
That it was time to pluck the last of the apples and time,
too, for lamps and quilts, an end to all activity and related
things . . . He began to tremble with excitement.

"In January," he said, "I shall read *all of Cicero.* I *swear*
it."

She clapped her hands and grinned at him with admiration. She still looked like a dot down there, but so, too,
did the city. Or rather, like a droplet of quicksilver that
had been flung into the valley and left to rust there. All his
life he had wanted to abide with Judy in Time's aftermath,
a thousand years upon the farm. And then to toddle on
down hand-in-hand to that same "Edge" toward which his
people had always been drawn when came the time to go
there and . . .

"Do what needs to be done."

"I can't hear you!"

"What needs to be done?"

"Apples!"

But prior to apples, they had a tenth-acre of potatoes
that must be pulled out of the cold, hard ground. His
practice was to scoop them up one by one with a pitchfork
and speculate upon those that most resembled shrunken
heads. Ignorance, he saw, and blandness on top of that—
he had fallen into a pessimistic mood when Judy came up,
tapped him politely on the shoulder and pointed out
where winter was coming in.

He needed one hour and twenty minutes for the potatoes and then fifteen more to carry them inside and se-
clude them in various places. He had changed his mind

about the readings he had assigned himself for the on-
coming months.

"To hell with Cicero, I'm going back to the Greeks. No!
Don't try to stop me."

In fact, she seemed more worried about the potatoes.
"Thirty-two. I thought we had planted more."

"Oh? Well just wait till next year. I'll plant so many."

"Lee?"

"Yes?"

"How much money do we have left? I mean really?"

But his attention was focused on the woman herself.
Seeing her like that, her cheeks impacted by the weather
and a big red sloppy ribbon in her hair . . . She began to
edge away.

"No Lee, please."

"Winter will have to wait."

"No, no!"

"Come, dear."

"The chum, Lee—he'll see us."

"Churl, you mean."

Thus Lee—he was running after his wife (who was fast-
er than he had remembered) when, just then, the dog
barked, thunder clapped, sun went down, and winter
came pouring in.

In earlier times, Lee had believed that all good things
are located in the mind alone; now, certain of it, he went
up to the third story and stepped out onto the covered
balcony where he maintained a mounted rifle of unusual
length together with some five hundred cartridges indi-
vidually wrapped in golden foil. Far, very far away, over
the meadow and down by the lake, a hundred-year-old
mansion had "slipped its moorings," as it seemed, and was
drifting ever so slowly toward the north-northeast. Focus-
ing on it with his glass, he searched each window before
then turning to the yard and garden, the two cars, the

sundial, patio, and birdbath. There, behind the wisteria, *that* would be where a notorious love affair had had its start, a stormy one that had waxed and waned over the years, pursuing its course in Europe until the two of them had finally had enough of it and the thing had abated down at last to nearly nothing. As to the woman herself, that was her sitting in the garden in a wide-brimmed hat. Eighty years into her age, she seemed unaware that winter had just come in.

Slowly, maliciously, Lee unwrapped one of the cartridges and put it in the chamber where it fitted extremely well. (The foil he saved, expecting to find a use for it later on.) In his neighbor's field, young horses were plunging jubilantly through the weather, but neither upon them nor upon the woman did Leland aim his weapon. Nor did he care to fire upon his own dog, nor shoot at hens, nor use his telescope for looking over the boy's shoulder to see what he was reading, nor shoot at him, nor anything else *except for the city itself,* which had so many target-like qualities—upon this he most certainly *would* take aim and fire, and gladly, too, and did. In this way squandered Lee sixteen precious bullets upon the upper city, and seven the lower.

She had made for him, his wife had, a fine numble pie, and allowed him to sit in her lap as she fed him with a big iron spoon. Lee, meantime, had put on Walton's violin concerto, "Judy's song," he called it. Drawn forth from his habitation by the music, he expected at any time to find the chum pressed against the window with his ears on fire. But as for Lee himself, who believed that all the really good things occurred in his own mind alone, he found that he was in danger of falling off to sleep while still at table. Suddenly, out of the silence of the night, his wife said this:

"Couldn't I see the money, Lee?"

"Say what?"

"So, I'll know how much we have!"

"Oh, for goodness sakes."

He had to go throughout the house—the money was here, there, everywhere—and then bring it to her where she sat in candlelight wearing a worried expression. Closing the curtains, they divided their wealth into bonds, cash, foil, and some six pounds of heterogeneous coins among which the woman immediately descried an old zinc half-cent piece larger than a saucer. Lee preferred the bonds, serious-looking documents offering dividends to the owner together with a stately portrait in black and grey of President Davis.

"These are no good, Lee," she said, touching them politely. "They just aren't."

He could feel his gorge begin to rise. "*These*," he said, gathering them unto himself, "are bonds. *Bonds*. They represent a stake in the future."

"No, Lee. The past."

"Same thing! It's the same thing! Read Toynbee." He stood and walked about the room. His wife, "the Divine Judy," as they called her, was retreating into her pragmatic mode. "Hey!" he said, "want to take a little stroll down to the lake?"

She did not. Instead, she had spread the bills of cash across the table and was reading them worriedly, reading them twice, dismayed by the story they told.

"Lee. Is this all we have?"

"No, we have the bonds. Which is not even to mention the money we get from renting him out to the neighbors; don't forget that."

"Lee, Lee."

"Well what am I supposed to do! Christ, I strive all day, striving and thinking. And who takes care of the churl, hmm?"

"I know, I know. No one could do better—I know that. And someday people will realize it, too, and be ashamed of the way they behaved."

"Oh sure! When I'm rotten and dead."

"It's always that way, Lee."

It calmed him. He was thinking of Poe and others in the spiritual line that had now come down to him. Next, he called for his chocolate milk and as she went to fix it, allowed himself to think about something Parkman had said about the Iroquois-Huron wars.

The milk was good, as was everything that came from her hand. He reserved the marshmallows for last.

"What are we going to do, Lee? We don't have even a thousand dollars."

"*One* thousand? And yet I can remember when we had nineteen. No! Nineteen *thousand*, I mean. Good Lord, $19 wouldn't do any good."

They sat looking at each other in the little bit of light that came from the rather slender candle that he had chosen to sacrifice for this interview. It made his wife beautiful, she who needed no such artifice in his eyes. "Ah, love," he said, keeping the words to himself, but adding then:

"Couldn't we go, you and I, down to the Edge one more time and grab for comets passing by? Yes, I know it's late."

"All right," she said.

Seven

Winter had seven parts, each part several phases; rising early, he tiptoed to the blue room and bent down tenderly over the recumbent dog whom he had at first supposed to be a pile of books. Each phase endured several days or, in one important case, moments only.

Carrying the radio in an empty shoebox, he retreated deeper into the house. It pleased him to hear about the kind of weather that bedeviled other regions, but especial-

ly *North Dakota*, the most awful, most flat, and most inquinate place along the dial. Maneuvering with delicacy,
he tuned next to a small town in Louisiana where an agi-
tated man was reading from the Book of Daniel. Lee gave
heed to it, which is to say until the transmission began to
peter out and was shortly superseded by the sound of
someone calling desperately from an even more remote
position along the time-space continuum.

Running from the intrusions of moonlight, he took up
his pallet and moved to the back of the house. Some sort
of tumult had broken out down below in the city; he could
see flares in the sky and long lines of cars headed out of
town. Heart pounding, he waited for the explosions—
might not *this* be the moment he had so long waited for?
That the people, bored at last with stocks and bonds, had
agreed to slay each other at 5:45 that very morning?
Thrilled beyond measure, he raced for the telescope but
ended up through a series of errors with the rifle instead.
There was no doubt that *something* was taking place below, but whether it were rioting, or merely dawn, or
whether the overload of ignorance and bad music had finally proved too much for the once-lovely earth any further to endure, he remained unsure.

Outside a certain amount of dew had fallen. Lee hurried forward across the yard, striving to keep the hem of
his robe from dragging in the stuff. The monster, he discovered, was asleep, his face covered with an open book.
Using this opportunity, Lee crept closer and gingerly lifted
the boy's cuff, horrified anew to see how the device, a
thing so primitive, had engrossed itself in the living flesh.
"Yes, it's uncanny," he said suddenly, filling the chamber
with his voice and bringing the boy to his feet, "that a person could fall asleep with that particular author, who never induced any sleep certainly in *me*."

The child was horribly embarrassed. Lee waited with
increasing impatience as, first, he gathered the book off

the floor, folded it, and then sought about for the most suitable place in which to set it down.

"How long have you been with us now, Reuben? And your gestation, is it one-third finished would you say? And are you one-third wise?"

The boy looked down.

"And ready to do what needs to be done? Hmm? And Reuben, do you sincerely believe that high things are high and low things low, and higher is better, and all men are utterly unequal? And do you adore what has been done in Europe and especially Greece? Well, do you? And that power properly belongs to those only who have no peers?"

The boy looked up.

"No! No friends for thee! And no woman neither."

(The monster groaned and moved back into a corner of the room, sulking now.)

"No, for thee, Reuben, no woman is in store. I *am* sorry, truly I am. For they've all gone away, my friend, or turned into men. And won't be coming back neither, not for another hundred years at least. But listen to this—your brother's grandson, if he be lucky and you for your part, if you carry out what must be done, perhaps in the process of time *he* at least might come up against someone who might almost be like Judy!"

The boy was not consoled. Lee waited as he went deeper into the corner and then turned and glared back with one grey eye. It was hard, nothing could be harder, than to send him forth to wander at large through a world that no longer had women in it, never to be given a chance at love.

"I *am* sorry. But never hesitate to *use* them, child, and do to them whatever you want. Are you writing this down? And now for the cities—they'll have to be removed, every last one. Oh, I don't say it'll be easy. But *they* set them up, and *they* can take them down. No damn cities under the sun!"

The youth came part way out of hiding, his face luminous from hearing about cities coming down. Lee took note of that enthusiasm. "You'll go far, boy, riding to power on women and girls. But tell me, have you begun your study of the German tongue? You're going to need it, my friend, if you're really serious about extending your purview into Europe. The West is old and wants to die. So. And now would you care for a little bit of chess?"

He rose, went to the cabinet, and took out the board and players. Knowing the boy's preternatural ability in this game, Lee apportioned to him the black king only, and a few random pawns.

Eight

Black, too, was Leland's mood when he began to trek back to his own quarters, knowing full well that dawn must come ere he could reach there. He called attention especially to the south-southwest, where crowds of birds were pecking at the rubble that not so long ago had been the moon.

Thus Lee, so broken and bent over from games of chess that he did not immediately recognize his own wife when she emerged from the house dressed in a suit of some kind. Thwarted by her own high heel shoes, he had no trouble chasing her down.

"I see. Fifty-four years of marriage, and now this."

"Oh, don't be ridiculous."

"Fifty-four! But really dear, you didn't need to get all dressed up just to run away from home." (She had gotten into the attic trunk apparently, and taken his grandmother's hat, an unusual object last seen by him in a hundred-year-old photograph. That was when the truth crashed in upon him.)

"You've taken a job!"

She said something.

"I can't hear you."

"Yes!"

"Great Moses, she's going down into the city!"

"We have no money, Lee! We don't."

"Work for an employer!"

"Please, Lee." (She continued to glance at her watch.)

"You know what *they* are, don't you? Bottom line? Cash flows? But just you wait, Reuben's going to deal with those people when he gets big, oh yes indeedy, and I mean *deal!*" (He made a slashing movement that failed but by an inch or two of knocking off her hat. She had been more than five feet tall at one period, but in recent years had given much of it back. She was still of course a beauty in his and most peoples' eyes, however miniaturized her present condition.) "Ah love, the guillotines shall feast in truth on that great day when at last . . ."

"I've got to go, Lee."

". . . blood."

"Please."

His authority had waned since those days when he had himself frequented cities and, sometimes, had brought home money from them. Horrible and horrible it now seemed to him that such a one as she should have to go to town in a foreclosed car while dressed in the way that she was. Horrible, and yet not quite as horrible, from his point of view, as if she had chosen to run away from home. Comforted by this, he went inside and after taking down two books and peeping briefly into each, poured a drink, got into bed, and began dialing back and forth astutely on the radio.

Nine

There followed a period of about six weeks during which the lout went from gestation to gestation, growing larger. Lee almost dreaded to go outside or to the barn and risk finding some new thing—a computer made from bicycle parts, a beautiful woman sculpted out of what till yesterday had a been a landmark pine. Accordingly, he retreated ever more deeply into the house, waiting for this winter finally to end and the next one to begin.

But the nights, ah the nights were his. He used to rise up after everyone else was in bed and, taking his telescope with him, creep on down to the Edge and wait there until such time as his wife might join him. Too tired, too exhausted, and too sleepy to use the spyglass herself, she trusted in his descriptions of what was going on in the city.

"You work too hard," he said, "and bring home all that money. There's no question but that I shall burn for this someday." And then: "Oh look! Two trains have collided in the middle of the city!" He fancied that he could see urbanites dancing in the flames and could hear their screams, and that this in turn had set off the dogs passing the news from hill to hill.

Finishing his brandy, Lee got to his feet, led his wife a safe distance from the Edge, and scattered pine needles on her for the warmth. Not far away—Lee jumped back—the boy had taken up in an "armchair" of stone destined twenty years later to be known as "Churl's Throne."

"You come here," Lee said to him, "And someday this whole province will be yours, that entire area between the Chatahoochee" (he pointed to it, a sterling river than wended in and out of the iridescent counties) "and the Cahawba, too. O child, child, if only I had my youth again, and a mentor such as yours!" He pointed to the Atlantic and the Pacific and the space that lay between them. "But are you the one for it? To take the Democracy and break it like an egg? It lies in the gutter, boy, the Western crown. Will *you* be him who picks it up?"

The monster was not an arm's length away, enabling Lee to read the titles of the four books that he carried always. "You've read enough," said Lee suddenly.

The boy turned and looked at him with morbid eyes.

"Want to end up like me? No, no, if you go on *reading*, why then you won't *perform*. And so just hand over those four books of yours, yes and the fifth one in your vest. Otherwise you'll soon be needing glasses."

Instead the churl stepped back two more paces. The older man would need all his suasion to turn the boy around and sit him down and make him listen and then stand him up again and send him off on his long mission. "All my life," said Lee, "I have considered beauty to be the best of all things. Therefore, they hate me." (He pointed down into the city.) "All right, not many people actually *hate* me. They would though, if they could. And if they knew who I was."

It was a delicate moment, fraught with meaning for world history. Lee imagined the boy saying, "You've ruined my life!" or something of that kind, although the wind forbade him from actually hearing anything. Guessing at what the boy had said, Lee replied:

"It were ruint ere you arrived here."

That was true. Recognizing the justice of it, the boy limped off sullenly, moving further down the Edge until at last Lee had to cup his hands and actually yell into the direction in which the boy had disappeared.

"Your role is clear!"

No answer came back to him from out of the dark.

"The Democracy grows old, old and rotten, a paradise for mediocrities and needs to be brought to an end!"

He slept briefly, Lee, and then woke to find the churl sitting nearby with both his good and bad legs dangling over the Edge. He had brought the cello with him but was playing too softly to annoy the hens.

"My wife is forced to drive a seventeen-year-old car. Does that seem fair to you? Works all day, she does, and yet is only x inches tall. How tall are you?"

The youth did or did not say something; Lee couldn't hear it.

"Yes, it's pleasant to take advantage of other peoples' books while siphoning off their hard-won knowledge, very pleasant indeed. But now the time for that is ending and . . ."

The varlet groaned.

". . . and very soon you must reintroduce yourself to the real world where alone honor can be won. Here, I've made a list." (He handed it over, a three-page schedule with glosses in the margin.)

He could see woe in the boy's moon-enhanced face. Lee almost felt badly about him, thinking of the severe trials that lay along the path to power. It was while they were swapping the pages back and forth, each man trying to foist them off onto the other, that one sheet fell out and began to fall away, dropping ever so languorously into the valley where someday long years after the city itself had turned to dust, a passing shepherd was fated to pluck it off a thorn and scratch his head and then set off reluctantly to carry out what still remained to be done.

Ten

He was disappointed to find that the boy, in his search for warmth, had formed a poncho out of a seventy-year-old horse blanket taken from one of the chambers in the barn.

"I'm disappointed," Lee said. "I thought you were harder than that."

The boy said nothing. They were both so busy, and the number of books so great that when at last they had been set up in the yard in the same approximate order in which they had stood on the shelves, at that point Lee began to have misgivings about setting them ablaze.

"I do believe I'll keep Murray's *Homer*," he said, never mentioning that he had two further copies in the house. "And look, old Orosius himself in paperback—who would have thought it?"

The boy went on darting in and out of the flames, salvaging perhaps a score of volumes before Lee shut down all such activity by glaring at him severely.

"And here's a full set of the *Monumenta Germanica Historiae*! Ah well, certainly *I'll* never have time to read it all again. But why are you crying boy? You're supposed to be harder than that."

It was near to two in the afternoon before they had put together the second pile, an unsteady arrangement predominated by nineteenth-century fiction. Once again Lee came forward and after having snatched it away from the boy for the second and third times, returned the little wooden chess set to the flames. He continued however, the churl did, to hug to his chest his favorite recordings, obsolete performances worn down by now to an extreme thinness from too much listening.

"I'm *ordering* you to turn loose of those recordings," Lee said, "and that's an *order*."

Wringing his hands (man-slaughtering devices that could have done all sorts of things to anyone who thwarted him), the monster set off limping in a circle, as if the problem in his leg had been aggravated by this new distress. Lee made a concession:

"All right, you can keep *one* disc. But not the others."

He brightened. Lee watched with fascination as he sat himself on the ground and, changing his mind frequently, began to go through the albums one by one. And if Lee had many other books and additional music that filled to overflowing several whole rooms in the house, even so he still hated to drench with kerosene so many good things stolen at so much risk from so many northern outlets. It was his own youth he was burning, and the youth, too, of the youth standing just next to him.

"You, Reuben, *you* strike the match."

Now at last he did cry, a far-away sort of sound that, combined with the sight of him, his great hands hanging down, his two kinds of shoes, and his tears as big as fruits—very glad was Lee that Judy didn't have to see it.

Eleven

In the days that followed, Lee remained inside the house. He knew that winter must someday end, bringing with it a lessening of his mental concentration and capacity for original thinking. Therefore, he drew even deeper into the family mansion, and if he had a mission for the boy, he simply wrote it out on paper, put the paper in a jar, and left the jar on the windowsill.

He did still attend to his radio, the most fragile by far of all his sources of information. He carried it in both arms as he turned to face in various directions while dithering with the knob. Or he might sleep for two hours and then read for two more. Or carry out that same proportion in reverse. Or rise and go to the window. Or leave a message for the churl. Thus passed the nights until, with winter waning, he used to go and check upon his wife.

It was quite dark, there where she lay in a reduced heap beneath a quilt with holes in it. That it *was* she, he knew it from the two wee shoes parked side by side beneath the cot. Heavy beyond belief, he lifted the one that was in poorest condition and tried to prise apart the little leathern toes that had grown together over time. Next, he bent down closely over his wife's glass hand, an object smaller than a 3 x 5 card but larger than a dime. But as to that smallest of her fingers (and he had to strike a match to find it), it was trembling ever so slightly from the bad dreams that came to her each time she imagined someone was hovering over the cot.

But mostly it was the woman's face that held fascination for Lee. He loved to rub his cheek against it and then, working with subtlety, pinch shut her nose until such time as she chose to come awake. He counted to six.

"Lee! Lee!"

"Here, always here."

"What time is it?"

He honestly didn't know. And then, too, her voice sounded so strange, causing him to turn loose of her nose.

"Today—No! I mean it—today I want you to get a new pair of shoes. Yours are all consolidated."

"Oh sure, and what about the varlet? His are even worse."

"He's used to it. Besides, it makes him harder."

"Well how hard does he have to be! My word, he doesn't even have a blanket!"

"Ah, but he does, the bastard. He stole it."

"Like that car?"

"We need it, dear."

He waited for the reply which, however, never came. Instead, to his horror, he saw that she had turned her back on him and was near to falling off to sleep again.

"The dog," he said slowly, "he appears to have disappeared."

That did it—she came awake at once and, climbing out of bed, began buckling on her shoes.

"But now he's back," Lee said quickly.

"Oh."

"And so, I suppose you'll be going back to sleep again?"

They gathered in the kitchen, Lee did, while the woman mixed the tea. He said nothing about her hair (disorganized), or that her robe was wrongly buttoned, not until

she spilled the tea and then got down and began daubing
at it with her hem.

"Hey, you're not supposed to do that!" he said.
"Smirching your robe."

"Oh Lee, I had a dream. A bad one."

He could not but smile. "Yes. Dreamt someone was
bending over your cot."

"No, worse than that. Oh, Lee."

At times like these, he would have her sit in his lap and
tell him everything while he bounced her up and down
and stroked along her back. She was not so heavy, no
more so than the first time he had cajoled her into this
position, years ago. He let her stay quiet for a few moments, and then:

"Oh Lee, it was awful. I dreamt about a great big tree!"

"Hmm, tree. Yes. And yet I've had much worse dreams
than that."

"But it wouldn't stop growing and growing, and just
growing!"

Lee now became more interested. "Growing till it over-
spread the world?"

"Why, yes." (She made a cup of her hand and pointed
into it with her index finger.) "And growing!"

"And that it grew up through the clouds? Knocking the
sky all to one side?"

"That's true. And just kept on growing!"

"Until it overshadowed the continent, did you say, and
most of Europe?"

"Yes! I guess so."

"Horrible! And blackened out the sky?"

"Lee, you're bouncing me too much."

"And China? Tell about China."

"Please Lee, I have to get down now."

"Joined with the sun, by Jove. Higher and higher with
roots in Alabama. Well! we know what that means, don't
we—when great spirits expand beyond control? So it was,

they say, with Assurbanipal and others in that line. Fee, fi, fo."

She was gone, gone to her chamber where Lee could hear her putting herself into order with a comb and earrings and other accouterments, soon afterward to emerge—(himself, he went on bouncing)—as a latter-day Penelope or Héloise, or something similar to that kind.

Twelve

"Your deep souls," said Lee (they were in the field) "hate change. They see it as a distraction and a nuisance for anyone who cares about important things."

The boy listened. All morning he had been breaking up clods of earth with his enormous hoe, until the noise of it had at last awakened Leland and pushed him out of bed. Still half-asleep, he emerged in a shirt and tie and pajama bottoms. He had managed to get into one of his shoes, and the other one, too. No use to call for breakfast, not since his wife had begun going down into Birmingham, there to fritter away full nine hours each day in an oat-meal-colored office building with antennae on the roof. Many times, had he sought for her there, always at the last instant to clap his hand over the muzzle of the telescope when he saw the quality of the people who drifted in and out of ken. Anyway, it would kill him, he believed, to find his own beloved wife tethered to a desk and made to share in some of the preposterous activities that had grown so popular these last hundred years. (He could not remember whether she were engaged in public relations work for a consulting firm, or whether consultancy for a lobbying effort on behalf of advertising companies involved in public relations.) Today his spyglass seemed especially drawn to tired-looking women who, most of them, or the best of them anyway, had far preferred to be at home on the farm. Just now he was examining a young woman of perhaps fifty whose face and boredom without end told him all that he presently cared to know about this century and what it had come to. A milkmaid she might have been, a bee mistress, or tavern keeper's daughter, any of which were better than *this*.

"It's impossible," he said, "to return the world to a previous period in history, and Toynbee says so, too. Nevertheless, that's what I expect you to do."

This time the boy expletived out loud in a kind of final exasperation and threw his hoe down.

"But I don't expect you to do it all at once, good Lord no. Why a few more years of *this*"—he inclined his head in the direction of the city—"and they'll come to you of their own choosing, demanding to be put to sleep."

The child muttered a word or two and then, showing further signs of a resentment that Lee had not previously seen in him, began to extract the little green peas that only moments ago he had been sowing in the field and began to hurl them ferociously one by one at the horizon and the sun. Lee turned his gaze upon him. The older man still had more books and music to his credit than the boy could cite on his own behalf.

"Ingrate! Have you forgot your obligations to Judy, and to me?"

There were other peas visible along the row. Marching side by side with him, Lee continued his harangue as the boy went back to planting the little objects in the proper way.

"Yes. What we see here in America is the absolute triumph of quantity over quality. And that's why *your* quality has to be larger than *their* quantity. Now I want you to continue this row of peas all the way down to that low-lying series of hummocks yonder where seven of my ancestors lie dreaming."

They both stopped and looked in that direction. As to how the boy was to accomplish all this and restore the ancient constitution, break the cities into towns, set up opera houses, and keep the wealth out of ignorant hands, how to carry out such labors and bestride the Atlantic on legs of unequal length and do it soon . . . It made Lee tired to think about it, but also glad that his own work was nearly finished now.

He spoke no further that day. Leaving the boy to his labors, Lee came inside and was well on his way to bed when suddenly he understood that winter had ended, bringing in its wake a long and tedious wait before it would agree to come back again. He did so dread it, the arrival of good weather and the sounds of noise as the usual low-grade people came bursting out of the city in order to contaminate with their persons the roadways and long-ago-lovely hills. He trembled for his wife and his books, but especially did he tremble for his churl lest the people come and poke at him before his time had come. He knew them! Yea, and knew the hungers that drove the Democracy ever onward toward more perverted forms of music and television around the clock. Spring was coming in.

Because she had returned from the city with her usual cheerfulness curtailed, Lee strove to keep out of her way. But when at last it came to be ten o'clock and still he'd been given nothing to eat, that was when he went and knelt down next to her cot and tried to get some conversation out of her.

"Well!" he said.

She turned slowly and gazed at him.

"The garden is planted, almost. Assuming Reuben ever comes back from Atlanta."

"Atlanta?"

"Why yes. I had to send him on a little *mission*, don't
you know." (He winked twice and nudged her where she
lay.) "Nothing he can't handle. Hell, I could almost do it
myself. So. And how was *your* day?"

"Oh Lee, these people, they . . ."

"Yes, I know."

"But they're very polite."

"Certainly they are! And well-dressed, too, I'll ween."

"Oh, Lee."

"Ignorant of everything, but full of expertise—am I   ·
right? I *did* warn you."

"They have *relationships*."

"Jesus!"

"But they . . ."

"They don't really like each other very much—is that
what you want to say?"

"It's so *horrible*, Lee."

"Yes. Now my grandmother, to take one example, was
an elderly woman, and yet she could have sliced to ribbons this whole generation with her pruning knife. Want
some wine?"

He ran for it and after pouring himself a substantial
drink, threw on some of his favorite music, nineteenth-
century stuff, the twentieth's only antidote.

Good with ladles and good with spoons, they reached
across the table to exchange samples of various things.
Invigorated by that, Lee then shoved off, going from one
piece of furniture to the next until in process of time he
came upon his favorite section of the house, a dark pre-
cinct with numbers of good books in it. It was here he had
placed his best couch, a calming influence covered in
cowhide. For him this was by far the best part of the day, a
time of napping and digestion; he liked to lie there for an
hour or so, scripting in his mind the dreams he planned to
unfurl later on. Herself, the woman had found his grand-

mother's glasses, an heirloom with gold frames and very thin lenses, and was sewing studiously in the almost insufficient light of the paraffin lamp. Would only she might turn a few degrees in his direction, then would he be able to spy upon her from his favorite angle; instead, the lamp began to sputter and then, finally, went out altogether, leaving them with nothing to do but to step forthwith into those same dreams prepared by him with so much foresight.

Thirteen

They stayed that night in the yellow room, the most capacious in the house. But when in spite of his best efforts he came awake around midnight and found his wife curled up in a state of perfect unconsciousness, he lifted her up in both arms and spoke soothingly:

"All's well. And now we're simply passing through the kitchen on our way to the music room. But don't worry, dear, I'll be careful not to stumble."

"Music room?"

"Precisely."

It satisfied her.

"And dear, we'll be able to get that operation now, just as soon as the churl brings home the money."

"No, Lee, it won't do any good. I'll always be short."

Her special place was in the corner, where he set her down among her things. As a final measure, he called the dog and *ordered* him to stand guard for the next several hours, and never mind to which area of the house she might wander during the remainder of the night.

Himself, Lee went back to bed. All day he had been plumping for a dream about the sea, life on board a submarine for example, or a long journey in a rocket ship; instead, after a full quarter-hour during which his insubordinate mind continued to revert to more impractical things, he rolled and cursed and stood and went outside and micturated in last summer's roses. Only then did he truly begin to dream, having first returned to the basement where, however, the radio was able to pick up but two signals only, weak ones emanating from the same far-away township in an untraveled region of the nation.

He dreamt of hate, an essential part of his regimen that started out each time as a headache in his lower amygdala and then expanded to fill the room, the house itself and the world, stopping only at Judy's door. He knew what to expect from a dream like that, one in which all of history's "progressives" had been brought together in a narrow space, stripped naked, and glued to the ground. And then to deal with them appropriately, he would raise dead men from their graves, farmers, many of them, along with an appreciable number of confederate veterans.

Later on, thinking back on it, he was to remember that each such veteran had come with a blowtorch, pliers, extraordinary patience, and two spools of very fine wire. What followed, followed as always; indeed, one would have thought the whole planet was screaming. Of course, there were many other things that Lee saw, and much he could have written, had only there been readers to read it, and people worth sharing it with.

Fourteen

Morning came up brightly, accompanied by a dawn in which the sun was like the yolk and clouds the albumen of a giant egg that had broken open in the sky. Lee went immediately for his telescope but got no further than the next room before he perceived that one of the windows was crowded with Reuben's large silhouette. This time the boy was greeted with a warmth that on Lee's behalf was highly unwonted, if not unique indeed.

"Yes! By all means, do come in and so forth. The Divine will be more than glad, won't you dear, to make coffee."

She seemed strangely loath to leave them at just that moment, owing probably to her curiosity respecting the portmanteau that dangled from the boy's right arm.

"For me, the coffee should be well-sweetened. But black for the churl."

Again, she continued to seem reluctant. Humming patiently, he gave her another half minute or so and then drew the boy into the study and sat him down on a crate of as-yet-unopened books.

"Ah, so. Bad weather we're having, *nicht wahr*? And what do you have for us, I wonder, in that there little black valise? (Grinning, he went and touched it.) "Something good I'll warrant, eh what?"

But even at this late period the boy still had his eye on the shelves of books that ran back and forth across all four walls of the narrow room.

"Don't be looking at those when you're talking to me!" said Lee, using a sharper voice than he had intended. Meanwhile the youth had said nothing at all.

"Nothing at all? Well that's just the point isn't it? You *should* be speaking, and *now*. And where did you get those trousers, if I may ask?"

Everyone looked at the trousers, an ordinary sort of garment that, however (and it was the first time Lee had seen anything like this), fit quite well. Give him but another haircut, a new vest, and shoes that matched, and he might almost have been a better-than-average-looking man. No, Lee went further than that and began to predict all kinds of women and girls in this boy's future. Judy, meantime, had come into these private quarters without knocking and was again staring at the briefcase in a kind of silent wonder. He could see that she had prepared the coffee in some haste—it had not that spectacular quality that he expected in beverages that came from kitchens of hers.

"It's money," said Lee, "lots and lots of it."

Horrified, she stepped back two paces. Not so Lee, who had sent the rascal to Atlanta for just this purpose; chuckling, he began washing his hands in glee, an unpleasant thing to see.

"How much, Reuben, I say how much do you actually have in that satchel?"

The boy said something.

"But weren't they embarrassed to be taken like that? Come now, child, and spread the stuff on this table that we may see the visible results!"

And good results they were, too, comprising as they did some several thousand American dollars colored green. Lee gloated over it in his deplorable way, sometimes sniffing at the stuff, sometimes actually picking it up and sorting through it and, sometimes, lifting his glasses to read at close range the very tiny English words to be found in various locations, notable products of the engraver's art.

"You may well make a face like that," he said sharply as he drew out his wallet and threw some money in it. "These bills, these dimes and quarters, they stand in lieu of Judy having to go to town each day and do the bidding of some very fourth-rate people, philistines mostly."

That was true, and the monster could not deny it.

"They laugh at me because I have a radio and know how to use it. But how else was I to learn about all that rain in Iowa and Illinois? You see, Reuben, it's not necessary to do work, not really, not when you live in a country advanced enough to offer puts and calls on hog jowls and soybeans."

The boy noted it down and then, showing no embarrassment, began to reward himself with some of the largest bills of all, the foundation of his future success. Lee watched ruefully as the money, leaving his sight forever, went into the boy's vest.

Fifteen

With summer threatening, Lee went deeper into the house. Here, among books and photograph albums, he was almost able to believe that Time *had* after all turned about and was proceeding in a more wholesome direction. All such beliefs of course fled quite away when on clear nights he used to go on down to the Edge and dawdle there, watching what went on in the city.

One good thing—his wife was staying home again. Oftentimes he heard her in the kitchen singing to the dishes, or in the garden, or among hens. He still liked to pounce upon her from unexpected places, sending her off into faint screams that brought the churl running from the barn.

For summer, providing warmth, had added two more inches to the scoundrel's height. Looking up at his creation, Lee saw no softness in him anywhere, especially not so in those vermilion eyes. "Ride them," said Lee (referring to women and girls) "ride them to power. Take their husbands' wallets, if you can, and place your hands around their necks." (He could see how the monster's left hand in particular was ever and again opening and closing in a sort of agonizing slowness that set Lee's hopes soaring.) "You grow cold, boy, and taller, and never do you laugh."

"I never laugh," said Lee, speaking in the boy's behalf.

"And yet your grandchildren, or their grandchildren anyway, shall live in a world of tremendous inequality, where love and art can flourish. And it was *you* that did it, Reuben, always you. Ah child, child, we shan't be ruled by employers *then*, nor by the trash that comes out of universities."

And so thus Lee when on that day the boy came out of the barn carrying a little straw suitcase large enough but no larger than for his flute and two thin books. Lee gave thanks that his wife was strolling down along the river and would not have to witness the scene that follows. Meantime he kept on powdering the dog, using for that purpose a three-part mixture of his own concoction. It did surprise him that after all his teachings, that the churl still wore the preposterous little woolen cap in which he had arrived, a reminder, one had to suppose, of his origins in the hills.

"Leaving us!"

He blushed.

"And why not? After all, you've pretty well sucked us dry of any knowledge we used to have." Suddenly, without expecting it, he felt his gorge rising high. "And so, you're off to 'conquer the world,' I suppose. Good, good. And me, how come *I* never conquered it, hmm? I was here first."

It seemed as if the boy might know the answer, but Lee stopped him before he could reply.

"Conquer the world, you say! Or anyway the Western share of it. No, I wouldn't recommend that you trouble too much about Africa and Asia. I mean! what did *they* ever do that could hold a candle, hmm? Nor Latin America neither."

He nodded slowly. Lee could see in him, he who never smiled, high resolve joined to that ignorance of fear that gives rise to fear in others. And then, too, his gaze was so concentrated and grey that Lee turned to see what landscape the boy was seeing.

It was, of course, the sun. To die and be dead, broken into parts and drawn into the sun, this was the career Lee foresaw for himself. Most likely he actually yearned for such a denouement, provided he could take with him his choice—he asked for but one—of persons. Thinking of this, he lapsed into an odd smile, too crafty by much and unpleasant to look upon. That was when he saw that the boy had left him and, disdaining the high road, was trundling across the meadow toward the woods.

To say that "he did not look back" would be untrue. Lee, who never went anywhere these days without his spyglass, saw it clearly when the boy stopped and turned and ran his gaze over the farmhouse with its vines and gables and the turret where Judy dwelt.

In the afternoon, Lee returned to powdering the dog. Halfway finished, he stopped. This was *not* the same animal with which he had thought himself sufficiently familiar as not to end up doing his neighbor a favor, it just wasn't.

Sixteen

A brawny man, about six-foot-five, a thousand-dollar suit and girls coming out his ears, this is what it had come to. Seems that he had inveigled himself into the state university and after a degree in chemical engineering, had transferred over to the California Institute of Technology for further study eventuating in three patents and a paper on quantum computing applied to recombinant technology designed to disaggregate viruses in the Aab-D4 range. Not that Lee or his wife, assuming they had still been alive, would have understood any part of it.

Some fables end up proving to have been correct, namely that the lout really had been seen, and not by just one person only, lowering himself down into the city by means of a steel cable attached to the column of Leland's house. One would have thought him too large and ungainly for that, or that he would have fallen to his death before the second full day had gone by. Or that he would have been met by journalists, or by the police, when finally, he touched ground some two or three miles outside the eastern gate. Here he teetered back and forth for a few moments and then strode forward quickly to a broad highway carrying very little traffic at this late hour. Knowing nearly nothing of trucks and automobiles, he made no effort to catch a ride with any of them, choosing instead to direct himself toward the pale dome of light that gave away the city's actual position. He could make good progress on the smooth surface of the highway but opted to abandon it anyway in order to avoid the people blaring at him with their horns. He had read of this of course and had seen films in Leland's library showing analogous scenes with people chasing back and forth in cars while firing shots at one another. A good thing there was a ditch alongside the road where he could travel in perfect safety, provided he didn't object to getting his shoes and socks all wet.

He was entering society with just one liability only, that discontinuity of his right leg where the flesh had been shorn away by his father's tractor blade. Nothing embarrassed him more, nor so puzzled the specialists consulted by Leland's wife. One would have thought the flesh of the foot and leg would have to be joined at some point. This was the limb that now began to give out on him, forcing him to hop forward with each third step and then stop and rest very often.

He had $1,200 on his person and a .357 magnum Smith and Wesson revolver with chambers enough for eight cartridges. One cartridge, it is true, was "out of round." Even so, he believed he could fire rapidly enough to make up for that, should the thing refuse to do as it should. Of money itself, he held, as mentioned above, just slightly more than $1,200 representing his percentage of the gains Lee had made with livestock futures. On the other hand, his suit had been damaged during his descent from *Peflia*, that six-acre patch named by his guardian in memory of himself. As to the boy's personal appearance, he had lost three buttons and his once-paisley tie had broken off in such a way as to leave hardly more than two or three inches of it. Suddenly, that moment, he jumped back and fired two shots into a discarded beer can, the first time he had seen an object of that kind.

He had come more than halfway to the city when he happened onto an all-night gasoline station with a girl behind the counter. Reuben went to her, tried to smile, failed, and then handed over a $5 bill. He knew almost nothing about women, except that this one seemed to be afraid. Having asked, politely, for a carton of cigarettes, he remained calm as it became necessary to give the girl more money still.

He stood absent-mindedly, allowing the girl to view his abbreviated tie and hooded face that even up to the present time has never properly been described. Still calm, he ordered a dozen candy bars and this time offered more money than required. Two men had meantime entered the shop, an older and a younger, neither of them presenting any sort of threat to Reuben.

He noticed how they stood back, staring into the distance as he dawdled in front of the register. He gave them a few moments, went outside, and seeing that their vehicle was pointed in the right direction, climbed into the bay and tried one of his new cigarettes. It was a good place for smoking (the moon was high and three-fourths full), although the poverty of the tobacco disappointed him when compared to what Mr. Pefley had routinely produced on his few acres.

Probably he slept, Reuben. Later on, he was to remember the sound of conversation and then the two men gazing down sadly where he lay among tools and spare tires and other litter.

"We can give you a lift, if that's what you want," one of them said. "Shoot, we're going there anyway."

The night was chill, and the dog had backed into a corner. Lying face-up among the bags of feed, Reuben focused upon a bright golden star running across the face of the moon. All these objects were "moving away from each other at the speed of light," which was not the only of Leland's theories that he questioned! Impressed by Nietzsche's work, his mentor had striven to integrate into his own thinking the theory of the eternal repetition of the very same thing over and over again. This too, Reuben doubted. Certainly, he wished for no such repetition of his own early years, bleak days with ignorance all about.

They arrived at the city proper at about three in the morning and finding the eastern gate unattended, drove quickly into the heart of the downtown business section, a blighted area that to Reuben's eye appeared to have been set up in higgledy-piggledy fashion without any sort of advance planning on the part of anyone. He saw a two-story hardware sitting between buildings that were four times as high. The roofs were flat, most of them, and some were slanted, and all in all it seemed to him a civilization that cared very little for those things that Lee and he cared for most of all.

But all this faded away into absolute inconsequentiality as he went forward, peering into the businesses—insurance and mutual funds, pharmaceuticals and women's shops—that filled the block. Suddenly he jumped off to one side, leery of the automobile coming more or less in his direction. He never wanted to be in *front of* these things, especially when they seemed to be as many degrees off course as this one. Crossing at the intersection, he passed a man with a clarinet who had no audience, and then a cluster of black people—he had heard about this—who appeared to be waiting for him. They were wearing chains of gold, two of them, while the third person had dyed his hair a bright strawberry red. The last that Reuben wanted at this stage in his career was to be assailed in his weakest part and have his leg snapped in two. And then, too, like Leland, he could see *through* human flesh, a facility that informed him of the hideous glistening viscera that comprised the biologic person. Therefore, he continued forward, hoping to get past all this and return to his examination of the city.

"Hey, dude!" said one. "Where the fuck you think you going?"

"Shit, he don't know *where* he going. Hey, got any money asshole?"

Reuben looked down at them, them with their egg-shaped heads covered in "hair" that looked to him like a species of lichens. He despised them, then and always.

"He don't even know how to talk! Dumb mother-fucker. Hey fucker, where's all that money you was going to give us?"

He reached for his gun, Reuben, but then in a sudden excess of delight took the head of the strawberry boy in both hands, brought it low, and smashed his left (not his right) knee into the boy's pre-historical face. Silence followed.

Came next a series of three shops, all of them vending clothes for women. One specialized in shoes and hats, one in wigs, and another in T-shirts with obscene slogans on them. He had been in town not yet an hour (he who had been nourished on Medieval philosophy), but already he felt himself fairly well-apprised of the intrinsic quality of this especial epoch. He passed a dealership parked all around with German cars, and next to that a government office offering one-pound specimens of tax-provided cheese. Reuben, who had consumed nothing but candy bars, pressed against the window, his eye upon a tall, thin individual sorting through the supplies. He was willing to pay, Reuben, but somehow couldn't bring himself actually to tap on the glass for the man's attention.

The following block had been preempted by a four-story structure consecrated to national security issues. However, the windows had all been painted over, and Reuben could see nothing of what might be going on inside. Accordingly, he crossed to the other side and turned back toward where the strawberry boy was being lifted into a long white ambulance with bright blue and red lights flashing prominently into the night. The boy's friends—and Reuben took note of this—were nowhere to be seen.

But now dawn was arriving, a daily procedure adumbrated, as Lee had liked to say, by scads of corybantic fowl. He waited for it, staying in place until the rim of the sun nudged up behind the buildings and began to cast a rose-colored light deep within the stores. He passed a coffee shop with five untrustworthy-looking men hunched at the counter, the largest assemblage of persons he had so far witnessed in the city. The next block offered an all-night gymnasium in which he descried an already very slim girl pedaling frantically on a piece of equipment. Some, but not all, of these phenomena had been explained to him by his proctor; even so he could not fend off a certain dismay as he studied the merchandise arrayed with such care in the show windows that continued on for half a mile at least, if not even further indeed. He particularly studied the manikins and their facial expressions, which he assumed to be the national standard for these times.

It was 4:40 in the morning in Birmingham when Reuben committed the first of those acts that were to give so much delight to so many biographers, namely his attempt to climb to the top of the next telephone pole and take a whole view of the city and its arrangement. Thirty feet above the ground, he turned in the four directions, gaining all sorts of information. Startled to find a lofty statue of Hephaestus located several miles away, the two beings stared at one another across the distance. But the rest was waste, a mere jumble of undifferentiated homes and filling stations and shopping centers encroaching up the hillsides that encircled the town. There was no question but that the area was at last coming awake, particularly in view of the flood of automobiles converging on the business district. Some people were still asleep, others were having breakfast, while still others, policemen in fact, were waiting for him directly beneath his roost.

He was ushered to an automobile that was too small for him and carried at high speed down to a grey three-story building with people milling about out front. Next, he was photographed by a grinning man and then prodded into an open area in which some dozen persons, most of them drunk, were loitering along a row of benches. He exchanged glances with a black man of about his own size and weight, both of them refusing to look away until the other person did so first. All in all he counted four Negroes, a Chinese, and three short dark people who later on he was to understand had entered the country illegally. It angered him when a health enforcer with an indignant face came and took away his cigarette, an action that ruined the eye contest he was carrying on with yet another person.

He was learning a great deal and learning it quickly. A sound of yells and cursing came from deep within the building. Caught he then a whiff of bacon and coffee coming from the kitchen. Next to him a man was slightly bleeding, and next to that a tattooed woman sat gazing down into a pool of brand-new vomit.

He was summoned to the counter and asked, unavailingly, to yield his family name. He hadn't any. His revolver was impounded, his coins, his $1,200 in paper money, his cigarettes and candy bars, all were taken from him and placed in a cardboard box. Three men stood close by, obtuse-seeming people with rubber batons and guns of their own. He might or might not be able to prize loose one of those guns but wasn't so confident as to think he could cope with the whole crew all at one time.

Still reasonably calm, he followed down a narrow aisle between caged prisoners yelling at him. He saw a man on a toilet, a small white cat running down the corridor, a naked person exercising on the bars. He predicted, correctly, that he was about to be forced into one of those cells, a narrow compartment (about eight feet long) that already contained an elderly man with bits and pieces of a beard. At once that person drew off into the furthest corner and sat on the floor.

Left alone with no possessions and nothing to read, he tried, Reuben, to recite certain stretches of English romantic verse introduced to him by Leland's wife. Half of him was scientific and the other half romantic, and after ten minutes of poetry he began to visualize the atomic structures of the six most common bromide salts.

Seventeen

He endured sixteen hours in that narrow chamber and then on the following day was made to quit the place in favor of an abnormal person dressed in pantyhose. Not that he had wasted those hours! Later on, looking back on it, he was gratefully to remember who it was had given him a phone number that was to play an important part in the child's later career.

His candy bars were returned to him, as also some of his cigarettes and silver coins. But instead of $1,200, he found just seventeen $1 bills in his billfold, and even these were creased and worn. But mostly he regretted his revolver, never again to be seen by him.

He was learning a great deal and learning it quickly, and when he walked free at 11:20 that morning he was greeted, not by cheering crowds, but rather that same feature writer who wanted further information about his episode with the telephone pole. Instead, Reuben turned on his heel and strode hurriedly to the west, as if that were the best direction for food and water and mayhap a library in which to resume with Lee's reading list. He passed through a two-acre park, astonished to find pigeons pacing fearlessly among the benches. Even so, he proved unable to catch one. Instead he took several of his candy bars and after depositing the wrappers in a mailbox, followed up the candy with two cigarettes smoked in quick succession. It was a problematic environment, made much more so by the absence of toilet facilities. He entered yet another of the town's numberless dress shops and after walking back and forth jumped into a changing booth and urinated—he had no choice—against the wall. He hated to see the puddle he had created, especially when the woman in the adjacent cell began exclaiming at him. It caused him, that noise, to shut off what he was doing and then emerge half-unbuttoned into the midst of three shoppers posturing in front of a mirror that provided manifold images both of a woman and the churl.

He had no wish to be put in the same cell with the man in the pantyhose. Next, they tried to force him in with an albino of some sort who joined in protesting the arrangement. With four several policeman cooperating in the effort, they at last bundled him into a cage (several inches too short) furnished with massy bars and an old-fashioned lock that must have weighed several pounds. He watched, watched Reuben, as they gathered up the worst injured of the four men, held him upright, and assisted him from the room. Left alone, the boy then smoked a number of cigarettes and finished off his candy bars. The cage was well-

constructed, and never would he be able actually to escape from it by ordinary methods. Very different was the
ceiling of his container, a simple sheet of tin if not mere
plywood indeed. He needed only a brief time to get down
on the palms of his hands and, reaching upward with his
feet, push the lid off to one side and stroll from that place
to the sound of ambient cheering. One single policeman
was posted at the door, a man of mediocre presence who
wanted nothing to do with it.

Reuben marched to the end of 7th Street before coming to a wall where he could finish pissing. An elderly
woman stopped and watched. With the sun directly overhead, Reuben gazed in that direction, ardent for the Alabama heat that in past times had so often fueled his larger
deeds. He remembered for example the time he had carried a copy of Burton's *Melancholy* out into Leland's field
and read the whole of it in a single afternoon. The rattle-
snakes he had slain, the three-room home he and his father had built from borrowed lumber, etc., etc.

By 4:30 he had found a reliable source of sweet water in
the faucets of restrooms found in department stores.
Here, working surreptitiously, he filled an empty soft
drink bottle and put it away in his vest. After his last session in jail, he had just $3 remaining to him, along with
half-a-pound of silver coin. On the other hand, he did still
retain a decent supply of cigarettes and a pretty good
knife.

He explored the town, encountering women and children, a man or two, and a squad of overweight Negresses
encumbered with jewelry. These he followed for a short
distance, intrigued by how they slid forward without ever
actually lifting their feet off the ground. At the corner of
12th and Marigold he perceived a spate of Latin American
immigrants—he thought at first, they might be the traditional redskin Indians of which he had read—redskin im-

migrants exposing facial expressions of surly discontent. Interested in everything he saw, he dallied in front of a hair salon, a video rental, a weight reduction workshop, and some four or five tanning salons. By now the sun was just two finger widths above the buildings, a clue and a suggestion that darkness would be coming much sooner than it should. He therefore turned in at the first hotel and after taking out his three bills and allowing the man at the desk to look upon then, used hand signals to express his desire for a room. But instead of replying, the fellow gave back the money and stared for a long time at the remains of Reuben's tie.

On his second attempt, the varlet entered a run-down sort of place and strode past the receptionist, who appeared to be asleep in any case. The corridors were long and dark, and every room he tried was locked. Finally, having mounted to the fourth floor—(he had never in his life been so far up in the air)—he found room number 476, a number easily remembered on account of its historical association. The bed was short but wide, the opposite of what he needed, while the faucet water was not as sweet as some he had tried. He observed a tennis racquet canted in the corner and a dark brown suitcase that proved to be locked. It did have a view, that place, which permitted him to look down onto the roof of the next building where he perceived a variety of litter—bottles and jars and the corpse of a cat. The city, he would have said, was a grey accretion formed of metal, asphalt, and glass. He saw the pages of a newspaper blowing down the street, a man in a hat, and other human beings spilling from a bus. He smoked, Reuben, and then dropped the butt in the "toilet" so-called, a commonplace appliance seen previously by him in more places than one.

He tried the bed, but then shortly got down on the floor and slept well for just slightly less than an hour and a quarter. The stink here was mostly of cleaning fluid. He

watched a little red beetle racing manfully through the
nap, a mountainous terrain with steep valleys. Someone
had dropped a penny but had declined to gather it up.
Holding it to the light, Reuben read the brief text that ran
around the periphery and then, coming closer, discovered
a tiny imperfection, a mere pinprick as it were, suggestive
of a flaw that must have developed in the casting. In any
event these were not the heroes *he* would have honored,
these Jeffersons and so forth whom he and Lee held largely at fault for the present crisis. Where was Epaminondas
for example, and where was Poe?

Over the past thirty months Reuben had absorbed a
great deal from Leland's radio; now, rising to his knees, he
switched on the television and began dithering with the
dials. Came first a blizzard of charged electrons and then a
commercial showing a skunk applying a certain underarm
deodorant. Came next a woman in a bathing suit lauding a
brand of automobile tires. A dog brushing his teeth—he
was learning a lot, Reuben. He waited for the program
proper, a comedy of two parents and four children tossing
scabrous insults at each other. He knew this much, Reuben, that had he spoken like that to his parents, *both* his
legs would now be bad.

He inched closer to the screen, intrigued that such a
disproportionate number of the actors were Chinese or
black, or hailed from Latin America. He had been warned
of this, of how the American elite used television to serve
social goals. Not only that, these people were shown to be
so noble-looking and tall and altogether more honorable
than your typical whites. Five minutes of it and he
changed over to the adjacent channel where a crime show
was in process. Here the murderer was rich, white, and
male whileas the detective was an impatient and authori-
tative woman barking instructions to her incompetent
assistant. Moving on, he alit upon a channel showing

three people in bed followed soon after by a newscast featuring a blond with prominent breasts.

He tried to read, but all that he could find was a pornographic magazine left between the sheets. The last he wanted was to be caught by the law while in possession of a thing like that. Immediately he slipped it under the carpet and never took it out again.

He slept briefly and then went to the window and looked down into the modern world, a treeless waste of consultants and public relations experts. Thus far he had seen just one dog, no geese, no horses, no little kitchen gardens nor fishing ponds.

He was awoken at about 11:25 by a tall man with a key in his hand. Reuben arose and went forward, waiting for a communication from the fellow. He was weak, that person, and his eyes set much too far apart. His breast pocket contained a tin horn and on his head was a party hat.

"Ah!" he said. "Sorry. I thought this was my room."

Reuben said nothing.

"And yet the key seems to fit. Strange."

Given no further information, Reuben (still half-asleep) came to his feet, shut the door, and went back to his impression in the carpet. His dreams, if he was having any, would have offered some very interesting subject matter to his biographers, but were never revealed by him.

At 8:05, having used the razor and toothbrush left in the bathroom, he was in process of exiting the building when he was stopped by a middle age European American blocking the door.

"So, *you're* the one," he said. "I'm calling the police."

Wanting nothing more to do with the police, Reuben didn't immediately reply. A second man, the same person as had burst in upon him during the foregoing night, stood off to the side wearing a belligerent expression.

"'Less you want to work it off. I let people do that sometime. Work it off."

"Lot better if you put him in jail," the second man said. Fifteen to twenty, something like that."

Instead, accompanied by both men, Reuben was escorted down into a sub-basement notable for the sheets and towels and pillow covers scattered about in front of an enormous and very noisy washing machine full of yet further towels and the like. The atmosphere was hot down there, owing no doubt to the array of dryers, all of them functioning at the same time. For a moment Reuben was about to opt for the police, except that he no longer had the funds for that. Accordingly, he stood patiently in one spot while the hotelier described the workings of the machines and the expectations vested in Reuben by the corporation.

It was bad down there, and the boy disliked having to come into touch with linens that had been used by human beings, including some who had probably been ill or Negroes, or who had resorted to this place for romantic activities. Where now were the leather gloves he had used for gardening on Leland's place? Next he tried to pack too many sheets into a machine that refused to accept that many.

"Trouble?" asked the man who had intruded upon him the previous night. "No, I feel real bad about this." He grinned.

The hotelier had gone away, leaving the boy in company with this supernumerary who was half Reuben's size and three times his age. Easy would it have been to resituate the fellow into the machine itself and tamp him down to half his size. No. Because that was when Reuben recalled one of Leland's last words to him, that a refined person ought never to violate the law. Instead he looked back evenly at the intruder, who suddenly volunteered to leave the building.

Never grant average persons leverage over their superiors—undoubtedly that was the reason Lee had recommended a strict adherence to the rules. And then, too, this was his first job of work, and he wished to do better at it than had ever been done by others. He studied sheets and pillowcases and how best to fold them, and towels, too. It is true that the two Mexican and one Salvadorian maid who made the beds were continually spying upon him, gratified to see an American reduced to women's work.

When came noon, he was given a meal of corn mash, collards, and baked beans with bits of pork fat in it. The coffee was good, pretty good, and he quickly swallowed three full cups of it. Across the table the three girls continued to titter at him while passing messages back and forth in the Spanish language.

French he could have understood or, given the needed dictionaries, Latin and Greek. One girl was fat, and the others lean, and between the three of them they ate almost as much as Reuben did. All was proceeding well, which is to say until the meal was finished and the eldest of the maids—they were maids, not maidens—until that person began issuing instructions to the best-educated whelp in the whole Southeast. Reuben paled, resolved that this would be the worst social position he would ever be willing to accept.

His supervisor was tall for her species and seemed to him somewhat shriveled for what might otherwise have been her age. He reckoned her at about five feet and ten inches while weighing not much more, he guessed, than around 120 pounds. Her shoes were red, her legs too thin, and her make-up, if any, had been so sparingly applied as not to be of benefit to anyone having to look at her. This was the woman he was expected to obey, especially when she stood back and watched with folded arms as he took up the napkins one by one and folded them in such a way as to hide the stains.

He had rather be reading, or doing irregular verbs, or scrutinizing at nightfall the permutations of the clouds.

He preferred to be fishing, or delving into Francis and Roger Bacon, or hewing wood. And never was he to understand why human labor had to be so unpleasant where large numbers live in proximity to one another.

He toiled for three days and on the evening of the fourth was pensioned off with a breakfast and $10 in cash and coins. Glad to see the last of him, the three mestizo girls waved him off with smiles and kerchiefs. In any case the bedstead had never been broad enough, or in his case long enough, for the whole group of them at once. He snored, they said, and every few minutes tended to thrash out violently with arms and legs. Having just turned twenty-four in age, he weighed somewhat more than had previously been the case, 272 pounds to be exact.

Eighteen

Thereafter he wasted two-and-a-half months as a warehouseman for a paint manufactory and then, once it had been discovered that he was a literate person and able to function in three languages, seven months more in an office job managing import/export receipts for the company's overseas markets. He was good at this, and by winter he was elevated to Accounting where he was taught the use of one of the only fifty or so quantum computers then in general release. His instructor was a blond woman who kept moving her chair nearer and nearer to him—he wanted to vomit—as the lessons went on, presenting him his first real problem with the members of that sex.

There were other women, especially after he had learned about suits and shoes and where to get a proper haircut. (His father, he knew, had never had a $50 haircut, and yet that man's wife had loved him to the end.) This too, he knew, that these people were wont to devote half their salaries to wardrobes, shoes, suntans, and hairdos. He used to watch them moving back and forth trippingly on elevated shoes, smiling betimes, casting looks at him. He got telephone calls. He lived in a world of short skirts, mascara, perfume, and hosiery. And then by age of twenty-five, he owned a car and had enrolled part-time in a branch campus of the state university.

His knowledge of the humanities was already extremely good, wherefore he was given a battery of tests and granted more than half the undergraduate credits needed for a degree. He studied chemistry (his favorite branch of knowledge) and by July had been partnered with a (Chinese) professor whom he disliked not quite enough to throw away the advantages offered by the association. His weakness, Reuben's, was in mathematics, which is to say until he signed up for a course designed just for him and two other students, one of them still another Chinese.

Moving right along, the university offered him a grant that was large enough to let him keep his car and hire a mistress, a black-headed woman of about forty already well known to the Chemistry Department. Later on, remembering his first interview with her . . . Truth was, he had been nervous on that occasion. It needed him a good ten minutes to describe (in his inarticulate fashion) precisely what it was he wanted. She laughed.

"We could do that," she said. "But I have about as much as I can handle already."

Probably he put on a sorrowful face, sorrowful enough to touch the woman's blasé heart.

"Jesus. Oh, all right. But you'll have to pay! Lots."

Reuben took out his billfold and let her peep at the contents, six months' worth of wages and scholarship money.

"Goodness. Well, I do have Fridays off. Afternoons."

He left his job in autumn, a wise move that gave him more time at the library. Reasons of thrift had put him in the town's worst quarters, a purlieu of drug dealers, gadabouts, and unleashed children without number. He used to go into the bars and look about at the Negroes, an incomprehensible race with jewelry, peculiar haircuts, and golden teeth. Thus far no one had offered him trouble— he was too large and had the face that he had. Even so, after a few weeks of this, he entered a pawn shop and invested in a revolver intended by him to take the place of the one that had been sequestered by the police. It was a heavy piece, each cartridge weighing as much almost as his also very heavy cigarette lighter. Back in his rooms, or room rather, he liked to aim it about at the people on the wallpaper, red Indians on horseback.

Far more difficult was it to acquire a silencer for the thing. He tried in two places, and both times was asked to leave the store. Finally, after traveling for about fifteen blocks, he came onto a repair shop specializing in vending machines and firearms parts. The craftsman himself was a bald man with an eyepiece affixed to his quartzite glasses. Speaking as clearly as he could, Reuben was describing what he had in mind when suddenly the man rose and went to the door and shut it.

"Illegal, silencers are. And why would you want one anyway? OK, never mind, you don't have to tell me."

Reuben passed over the gun and waited while the person took the needed measurements. He had all sorts of little instruments on his table, calipers for instance, and a hypodermic needle with its point sheathed in a cork. He had screwdrivers, some of them almost certainly too small for the human hand, as also a selection of glues and gold dust and medicines in peculiar-looking jars. On the wall Reuben espied an eighteenth-century engraving of an alchemist among his retorts.

"You can pick it up on Friday, round three o'clock," the shopkeeper explained. "But I'll have to charge you, you understand. More than you expect."

He tried but failed, Reuben, to say that he would be busy at that time. In any case his more immediate desire was for a holster that would be undetectable beneath a person's suit. But hadn't he passed a shoe repair just minutes earlier?

This, too, was a characteristic person who looked as if he had been stitched along his chin line and cured in acid over a long period of time. Reuben transferred the gun over to him, at the same time explaining what he required.

"Wait a minute, we're talking about a *shoulder* holster —do I have that right?"

Reuben admitted that he had.

"A shoulder holster for that great big gun you're pointing at the floor. But why—this is what I ask myself—why would a young fellow like you . . . Ah, well, you're the customer, right?"

Reuben agreed with that and then went on in his faraway voice to describe the sort of ornamentation he desired, a medieval symbol picturing an eagle flying aloft with a snake hoisted in its claws.

"I see!" the man professed. "And which are you, the eagle or the snake?"

By early afternoon he was back in the tutorial along with his (Chinese) colleague, the erstwhile girl who fancied herself a scientist, and a new boy with two slide rules dangling from his belt. Although not yet wholly adept in maths, Reuben had a preternatural ability to visualize nonsymmetrical molecules in three dimensions, never mind how tangled. Enjoyed, he did, imagining the latent properties of certain imaginary radicals never seen or synthesized before.

Nineteen

The boy was then "summoned," as was said, and sent forward to The California Institute of Technology, an arrogant organization that was good for his career but bad for everything else. Two weeks of it and it needed all the persuasive powers of his mentor to stop him from running back to Alabama again. There followed then about three months that has yielded no information to his biographers, no doubt an unhappy time for the child as he tried to adjust to the mindset of that state.

He saw them as the most advanced, most tanned, cheerful, and withal the most awful humans he had ever met. He used to arrive at meetings aforetimes and map out the exits and water fountains before any others came onto the scene. And communicated, when he must, with hand signals, or by tapping out the message on his computer screen. But primarily it were the girls, intellectual types—he loathed the sight of them—who came to him three and four times a day with trivial excuses for bringing him into conversation. He regretted his prostitute and tried (selfishly and uselessly) to inveigle her to California. On the other hand, the sea was nearby, and he used to swim out a distance before turning and looking back upon a country that seemed to be putrefying even as he . . . "Seemed"?

His economic standing, meanwhile, had improved to such an extent that he now had two rooms instead of just half that many. He might get up from his desk at an unexpected hour and then travel by foot to the kitchen, where he had laid away considerable reserves of canned meats, dehydrated milk, and sweet vermouth. His gun and ammunition he stored in a tin box attached to the underside of his enormous desk—save when he was carrying the thing in his vest. Books were everywhere. It is true that he had acquired duplicates of the best of them, some nineteen volumes that he had hidden away in various safe deposit boxes in Pasadena in preparation for the civilizational collapse forecast by Lee. And then, finally, he had stored up some 200 gallons of distilled water that over the course of several weeks he had concealed in the cold hard ground.

Apart from the ocean, he still had his German car, an excellent utility that suggested Europe might still have a future even if his own county didn't. He used to test it in the hills, moving around corners at unsafe speeds or, sometimes, sidling up threateningly to racial types and throwing back his lapel to expose his gun. Car, ocean, Negroes—these were pleasures that ranked equally with well-stocked laboratories and genetic engineering.

It was always human beings that he primarily despised. He saw them at the beach, pot-bellied individuals transporting several pounds of shit while striding past on stalks joined at hip and knee. As for the women and girls, they had come mostly for showing off their body parts, mediocre artifacts most of them, not worth looking at. Saw a man sipping at a beer, his facial expression proving him a true late-model American citizen. Had he rather, this person, be given a ticket to a hockey game, or hold in his hand an Aldine incunabulum of Aeschylus? And over there, it was clear enough what *that* one wanted, namely to have his dick sucked twice a day. He espied a child urinating through his bathing suit—Reuben was never again to come back to this particular ocean—and then a crowd of smiling young people all chortling at the same time. He wanted to slay the lot of them, making space for some better species that had already delayed too long. But first a cocktail party, and an invitation he dared not ignore.

Limping homeward, he was assailed by a girl in a sports car—he recognized her—who offered him a ride. The day was dry but fresh, fresh but the light got into his eyes. Nor could he read while having to cross so many streets and intersections while warding off the sun. His mind drifting, he began to think back on the beginning of things—Lee bending over him with a stick, the music, the test tubes, his godmother showing how to identify insects, the whole merciless curriculum that had made him the monster that he was.

He had two suits and nine ties. Had a pair of brazen cuff links bearing cuneiform inscriptions, the gift of some anonymous person who had wrapped the things in colored paper and left them in his mailbox. His shoes, no longer very new, were the worst part of him, albeit sufficient to the need. Finally, his socks, by far his most important accoutrement. He relied upon them, or upon one of them in any case, to hide those ten inches of uncovered bone that comprised the only weakness that he had so far discovered in himself.

He entered precisely on time and then strode to his major professor, a small brown Hindu with a Nobel Prize. They shook (briefly), exchanged a joke—Reuben could be terribly charming when called upon—and then went their separate ways to where the cocktails were being mixed by three nervous hirelings in bright red coats. He chose a vodka, did Reuben, based upon the fanciful label that bottle bore. There was no shortage of women in that room, post-modern types wearing their cunts on their sleeves. Some were "scientists," two were wives, and some mere opportunists looking for well-paid husbands with medical benefits. For a long time, Reuben said nothing before then continuing on in that mode for yet a while longer. Off to one side he saw a cluster of giggling youths sniffing one another's crotches, and nearer at hand a small brown queer with blistered lips. Reuben, who had often been pestered by these things in the past, warned him off and went for another drink. But even worse than that was the Academic Dean, a man with such a radical and transgres-

sive past that he'd been given a double salary. This was the
person who now directed himself in Reuben's direction.
His gait was swift, his hand outstretched, and his mous-
tache perhaps the lewdest Reuben had ever seen.

They shook solemnly for about eight seconds, a longer
period than it might seem when expressed in words. Finding nothing in the other man's eyes, Reuben lifted his
drink and consumed a portion of it. Thus far he had seen
no one in the whole auditorium whom he couldn't have
slain with his right hand alone.

"Well!" the Dean emitted. "Is this proving to be a good
year for you Reuben? Your project?"

Reuben did reply, using one of the generic phrases *au
courant* among gregarious people when half-drunk.

"But what do you do for *entertainment* churl? You
don't strike me as the sort to sit around and watch television all the time."

Reuben offered a non-committal reply. The man came
closer, his tone low, his mouth parts close to Reuben's ear.

"Yes, I know. It wouldn't be so bad, would it, if our
American society were simply worthless? Worthless would
be good compared to this."

Reuben looked at him, a man with half a million a year
and properties in Italy.

"Makes life hard, doesn't it, a culture as underwater as
this? Less than zero? Light years to go before we reach
mediocrity? Zero degrees Celsius? Come, I want to show
you something. Bring your drink."

Reuben, by no means unwilling to escape the chatter
and trash music, followed into the hall and then down to
the person's office, an unexceptional sort of space holding
an ordinary desk with what looked like ordinary papers on
it. He had three framed portraits on the wall of historic
persons whom Reuben admired just faintly, and in one
case not at all. Also, a periodic table holding information
that the man ought have memorized long ago. He was not

so tipsy, Reuben, that he couldn't have done real damage to this person in case he turned out to be just another California queer. Both men sat, both men drank, and each man offered the other a cigarette.

"One of Lee's people? Right?"

Reuben jumped back. He denied it of course and tried to change the subject.

"Not that you're the only one. Oh no, no, no, there's another fellow over in Wisconsin also trying to 'turn the world around.' Good luck with that. No, *you're* the one in the right place for that."

Reuben continued changing the subject while casting his eyes about the room. On the topmost shelf he observed a largish volume, very old, wrapped in shriveled binding. Opting to say no more, Reuben fixed his notice on it.

"Dead, you realize. Oh yes, and his wife, too. You were his last . . . *oeuvre* I suppose. You always carry that gun?"

Reuben didn't react.

"*Presumed* dead anyway. His body never found. A two-inch column in the *Birmingham News*. Human interest story about the number of his books. And the dog that fought so hard to protect them!"

He laughed merrily. Reuben's glass was three-fourths void by now, evidence of his developing immunity to liquor. He realized that he had been cheated in the exchange of cigarettes, a matter of *quality* as it were. That was the moment the man rolled his chair forward, putting himself closer to Reuben than Reuben wanted.

"Yes, well perhaps you *will* be the one. 'It always starts with one,' as Maudrepin claims. Lord knows, it can't go on like this much longer. Did I tell you we found three girls and two dogs having fun in the dormitory? Far too late in the day for pity, Reuben, promise me that much at least."

Twenty

He suffered from "punctuated evolution," another way for saying "in fits and starts." He might catch himself looking at girls, or falling to sleep over his books, or eating every day instead of the other way around. Or he might actually be tempted to the movies, but only to leave when the theater filled, and people began to turn up in his vicinity. He was weak, weak enough sometimes to skip his exercises, or resort to anti-depressants, or speak to himself when the lights were out. But he was strong, too, strong enough to have his television and his telephone removed, strong enough for 140 pushups and reading Schopenhauer in *fraktur*. Meantime his contempt increased, increasing rather by "fits" than "starts," higher than a ziggurat.

Example: he might catch sight of a routine American youth lounging in a shopping center with earplugs in his ears, tattoos, eyelids pierced, head full of shit. Those were the worst of times, when he needed every resource to stop himself from macerating the person in the spittle that came from his (Reuben's) two matched fangs. Or he might see an adult in short pants. Or hear a politician reciting yet once again the etiolated credo of Jefferson and the others, naïve people, ignorant of humanity's real nature. Or seize up a woman's novel and read a paragraph or two. Or catch a strain of tribal "music" emanating from a black person's car. Or glimpse at television. Or, or, or.

These were the times he would run to his second-hand German car and after dithering with the gears and positioning device and proving to himself once again that the thing had been put together by conscientious people, these were the times, he said, for driving out into the countryside. He liked to see the conurbation shrinking in the rearview mirror, as if the epoch of cities had at last passed away. Better still, he liked to imagine that the world had leapt free of its orbit, allotting twenty hours of darkness for just four of sun. Libraries and landscapes, pink purified oceans breaking into glass against the shores—these were the aspirations he allowed himself on better days.

Twenty miles out, he came up over a hill to find a dairy with numerous red cows facing off in all directions. Coming to a stop, he witnessed an elderly woman in a bonnet and stick trying valiantly to herd the cattle toward a spavined barn that had also been red at some date. It formed a pretty picture, green grass, bright cattle, windmill, and picturesque farm wife chasing up and down. He smiled, the first time he had done so since abandoning Alabama. More than smiling, he ended up leaving his automobile, passing through the fence, and then herding some half-dozen of the cows in the desired direction. The woman recognized what he was doing and together they shortly ran the animals into the barn and closed the doors.

"'Preciate it!" she said, coming into better view. "Whew!"

She was old enough certainly, and a little bit humpback, and her bonnet had no bill on it. They looked each other up and down.

"Don't believe I've seen you before," she went on. "Leastways not in that big old suit you got on. I got some apple juice in the cooler."

Reuben fell in line behind her. The house, in bad repair, was a traditional structure, two stories tall, high ceilings, wood stove—Reuben swooned—and holes in the carpet through which one could espy the hundred-year-old timbers out of which the place was formed. You wouldn't have found any "dry wall" in that place, nor circulating hot tub, nor marble fauns running through the yard. On the contrary, he saw only an abandoned grindstone and a tire hanging from a tree where about three generations previously little girls and boys were wont to swing—these were Reuben's usual assumptions in and around homesteads of this kind.

"Yes, they used to just love that old swing," she confirmed. "Dead now, most of 'em."

The juice was cold but had particles floating in it. Reuben would have preferred ice water but was too courteous by far to ask for it. Cold water from the bottom of a seventy-foot well with moss in it, just like the well he had perceived in back of the house. The juice *was* good, however.

"Yep, dead too," she admitted in response to Reuben's inquiry concerning her husband. "He used to farm *this whole land*, all the way down to Coldsmith Creek." And then: "Fifteen years, yep," in reply to the varmint's second question as to how long she had been abiding here all alone.

Together they fixed the little cups to the cows' nipples and then stood back to watch as their udders began to drain. Further down a massy bull was peeping belligerently from his stall, quite prepared to set upon anyone who might insult his wives. Reuben judged the animal coolly, confident that he could put the animal on the floor, if need arose. The barn had chickens, too, pestilential things curious about Reuben's leg. To escape them, the boy climbed to the loft and began to throw down an uncertain number of bales of hay. As to how the woman had been able for so many years to manage on her own, he couldn't explain.

"Oh, I get help," she said. "Sometimes." And then: "No, he's in Europe now. I guess. Anyway, he has his own family don't you know."

Reuben finished the juice, poured another, and finished it, too, and then after promising to come back someday, went to his car and drove anyway. It cannot be said that he was in a good mood, not after hearing about someone who preferred rotten Europe to life on a three-hundred-acre American farm. Exploring with his right hand, he discovered his revolver and toyed dangerously with the trigger before then taking a cigarette and in spite of the police, igniting it in full open view. On the other hand, his mood was rather good, the result of having met up with an actual human being, the first in ninety-seven days.

The second person happened just a mile or so further on, an automobile mechanic with a two days' beard and a greasy cap. Working hurriedly, whistling betimes, the fellow replenished Reuben's gasoline and filled the oil. It was this time that a black man came and parked and began using his horn peremptorily, as if he enjoyed summoning a white man to the needs of his car. At once Reuben took up his revolver and strode to the expensive (far too expensive) automobile driven by an African with a bone in his nose and a set of golden teeth. It wasn't necessary for either of them to talk; he needed merely, Reuben, to reach through the window, take the individual by the collar, and with the mechanic cheering him on, pound the top of the Negro's head four or five times against the ceiling of the cockpit. The technique was effective, causing the driver's two eyes to look off in non-coordinated directions, one here and the other over yonder. Meantime the muzzle of Reuben's revolver had worked its way about an inch or so up the man's left nostril, a yawning orifice as great in circumference as the Mexican 500 Centavo piece. As for the woman, the blacker of the two, Reuben took no action against her, not at that time.

"Lord!" said the attendant. "You done it! Shit that's what *I* should have been doing all this time!"

Reuben agreed with that and then followed the man to the kitchen where he was offered a glass of water with ice in it and the possibility of more. Came next a superb meal of barbecue, beer, and cold slaw, the first time he had allowed himself any sort of meat since Alabama. As to the wife, she was a worn creature with red hands, the sort who had exhausted herself in the effort to pay for other people's food stamps and aid to dependent children. Speaking in his modest far-away voice, Reuben conversed with her, a refreshing experience that, this too, made him think of the land whence he had come. He might almost be sitting on the front porch of his father's home, auditing the crickets whilst consuming iced tea. These two, husband and wife, though of course they couldn't know it, were to go down in his diary as the second and third good persons he had met in the course of a single day.

He drove into the evening, his eyes aglow for further people of the proper sort. But found nothing of that kind until at just after seven when he sped past a traditional little girl of perhaps four or five skipping rope in her parent's front yard.

With Ravel's piano music on the player, he came back to town in one of his most all-time cheerful moods. His thermos contained a quart of Sherry and Vermouth, two of the prettiest words in the language. Further, he had not had actually to use his gun (a box of shells now cost $30), his cigarette was long and flavorsome, and the music was as perfect as the composer could have wished. And then, too, he was driving into a dying sun of great beauty, a sack of granulated gold draining off into the sea by force of gravity.

His spirits were still good, pretty good, when he arrived back at the city and after taking a series of short cuts that alleviated somewhat the routine ugliness of the streets and automobiles, aimed for the municipal library. He had reason to believe the place was in possession of a copy of Du Cange's *Glossarium* in the 1678 edition. But first he must pass through the foyer, a considerable space with purple carpeting and crown moldings overhead. Today the display comprised some twenty photographs of dead people in progressive stages of decay, the work of a certain celebrated French philosopher whose own likeness was mounted on a tripod nearby. Reuben looked at it, his thoughts running back to other famous intellectual collapses of the ancient past.

The librarian was an earnest type, proud of her profession (the fourth good person he had met that day) who led him to the book and waited patiently as he tested the assumed quality of the Latin. The fifth good person was a wispy-looking introvert of some nature whose trembling hand wasn't long enough for the topmost shelf. Reuben gathered the desired item and after checking the contents, delivered it to the person.

"Much obliged."

Reuben nodded.

"I read these books," the fellow went on, "for the wisdom they may or may not contain." And then: "Of course *no one* could question the wisdom of Du Cange." (He touched Reuben's book with the longer of his two palsied hands, a movement and a statement that told a good deal about the person's mental development.) "Shall we go for coffee, you and I? There's a place nearby."

It was necessary to go down a flight of stairs and thence into an unornamented room of the usual dimensions holding six or seven tables with flowers on them. They settled near the rear and after exchanging cigarettes, spent a moment examining the seventeenth-century map of John Speed's London imprinted on the tablecloth. As to the people, and there were several of them, they seemed mostly engaged in staring at Reuben's bad place, which is to say until the boy had adjusted his trouser leg.

"I come here," the older man admitted, "to look at the people. People like you, yes and like that numbskull yonder with the face. After all, I've only got about five years for such activities." And then: "Yes, you could have been a real quantity, my friend, but for that bad place on your leg." And then again: "Actually I would have taken you for a scientist, to be perfectly frank about it. Instead, you're reading Du Cange."

Came the waitress bearing two cups of a foreign (and costly) coffee of some kind. Taking his flask, Reuben added an ounce of vermouth and a half-teaspoon of sugar. The place was full of Pasadenians eating food, an ugly spectacle endurable only because people had become hardened to it. He was astounded just then to see a white woman come into the place along with a lordly-looking male of the opposite race. Except for that, Reuben was in danger of getting bored. Impatient for books and solitude, he swilled down the coffee in some haste and then, pulling the candle closer, took back the volume and opened it.

"Hmm! He's begun to read even as we continue sitting here," quoth the introvert. "Strange. Would you care to know what *I've* been reading lately?"

But already Reuben had pounced upon certain scraps of marginalia (some in Greek) etched on the page in fading ink. Could ought be more entrancing than to find where yet another good person, the sixth that day, had put some really very percipient thoughts down on paper? He lingered over it, Reuben, allowing the divine odor of rotting vellum to travel to the brain centers of his head.

The Greek was good, the coffee too, and for a time he was able to immunize himself from the encompassing Americans talking excitedly of gasoline mileage and baseball scores. That was when his uninvited table companion offered him a card with his name and number and personal motto inscribed in glossy black ink. Reuben brought it up near to his eye where he could make out a wee little symbol in the upper right corner of the card, almost too tiny to decipher.

"We don't get many like you," the man said. "And someday, if I'm still alive, you're going to need someone

like me. Well! I'll say goodnight now. Be careful on your
way back to your small apartment."

They shook. The Americans at the adjacent table were
speaking now of quite other things having to do with tax-
es, tomorrow's weather, and the cost of shoes. Reuben
looked at them. He had no doubt that they still wished to
remain alive, especially the fat woman in the laughable
hat. But why? In the distance he could hear someone
laughing, and nearer at hand could sniff the vile odor giv-
en off by an emaciated girl in sixteen pounds of make-up.
He feared nothing, Reuben, except for ordinary things.
And that he had been set down by cruel accident at this
particular time and place.

He tried to pay his table fare, but only to be told it had
been covered by his erstwhile table companion. To atone
for that he left a largish tip, surprised to see the waitress
test one of the coins in her teeth. The moon was large and
though the city lights did it no favors, still conventionally
yellow. He strode hurriedly in the direction of his apartment, but then at the last moment remembered he had
brought his car. Two putrid youths were trying to prize off
his hubcaps, but very quickly relinquished the project as
Reuben drew nearer. Wanting nothing more to do with
the police, he declined to draw his revolver and stigmatize
the both of them with well-placed shots. Cars, the town
was full of them, beetling creatures running homeward to
unsatisfactory spouses. If only his paymasters knew his
forwarding address, it were back to Alabama for him.

"Why are we going this way?" asked the librarian, still
lingering at his side.

Reuben of course made no answer. It wasn't as large a
city as some, but even so offered a good selection of bowling alleys, pawnshops, tanning salons, and city buses full
of hanged manikins staring off in different directions. He
saw baleful Negroes loitering around street corners, a tavern with an immoral woman perched on a stool, an uphol-

stery, a neon lamp about to go out, a meek person with a loaf of bread under his arm, a dog in vain searching each and every passing face, a child, and then, just before he left off looking, an expert policeman practicing with his wand.

His own quarters were in a decent part of town, midway between the mansions of the rich and hovels of the honest. Here, at the corner of Hosbach and Peevy, he released the librarian and then turned just slightly to the east where instead of his apartment he aimed toward his favorite off-campus laboratory, a two-story structure to which he had only recently been given a key.

He loved the smell of chemicals late at night. A black man was in lab #9, a fellowship winner sent forward by an affirmative action officer with a sense of humor. Reuben moved past the "germ room" so-called, where the janitor was entertaining himself with the liquid hydrogen tank. His own lab, Reuben's was in peerless condition, his pens and pencils laid out in parallel and the glassware, of which there was a great quantity, as bright and transparent as if there was nothing there. Here, with no one watching, he sometimes spoke to himself in a rumbling tone that he didn't wish to share with others. Especially he spoke to a five-liter beaker full of a green "soup" in which two enzymes were working "against each other," as he explained later on. Five minutes having gone past, he left off speaking and tuned to the university's radio station where the second cello concerto of Shostakovich was coming to its most direful part. There were not probably more than five persons in all California listening to it, and the station itself was scheduled to be shut down. That was when his adviser, also so-called, came into the room and began congratulating the varlet for his late-night work:

"Well! Still at it, I see!"

Reuben waited to see if anything more was forthcoming from the man, and when he saw there wasn't, went back to working.

"Reuben, Reuben, Reuben, you really shouldn't smoke in here. Oh, and did I tell you you've been given a Ph.D.? Five votes to one?"

The boy drenched his cigarette under the waterspout and returned to his notes. His handwriting, imitated consciously from Da Vinci, was crowded with tidy little drawings of apparatuses, colleagues, and his own left hand.

"Reuben, Reuben, Reuben. What goes on in that head of yours? That's what people want to know." And then: "Christ, don't tell me that's your idea of music!"

Reuben smiled, or tried to. He was accustomed by now to the philistinism of his professors and had learned long ago to smile at it, or try to. In this case the man wore sandals and a salt-and-pepper pigtail that proclaimed his political affiliation. Reuben ignored it, or once again tried to.

"No one is perfect Reuben. Someday you'll understand that."

There was at that time a family-owned drugstore in the 500 block of Winton Road. Finding the place empty (it was four in the morning), Reuben purchased cigarettes and greenwort pills and in spite of his promise, a late edition Los Angeles newspaper with the picture of a rock star on the cover. He was in a decent part of town and his well-cared-for automobile made almost no sound as he wended among modest homes and tacit streets that conducted up into the hills. Were only the world always as lifeless as this. He wanted silence from beginning to end, and nothing left over but libraries, grocery stores, and a choice of guns and ammunition.

No one had entered his room in his absence nor perturbed the pens and pencils that lay in a pattern on his desk. He expected a two-hour grace period before the coming of the sun and traffic, an all-too-brief interlude which he should have devoted to his conspectus, but which in fact he wasted on the newspaper.

There was indeed a rock star on the front page and then, next, the photograph of a starlet in a bathing suit smiling back jubilantly at the Angelinos. He read a full half column detailing how a homosexual had been offended in South Dakota. Reading further, he saw the President had signed an urgent measure to redress the underrepresentation of black women in particle physics. And then, finally, at the bottom of the page, the not unexpected news that marriage contracts could no longer be restricted to just two persons of the same species.

The following page described some of the more interesting police actions of the previous twenty-four hours. He saw an officer standing between a great fat man and a crying child. One hundred twenty-seven "illegal" migrants had been captured at sea and hurried off to the downtown welcoming center where they were made to write full page apologies before given citizenship.

The following pages revealed even more. He found an opening for a human resources analyst adept in encryption bewareware but wasn't able to understand what precisely a person would have to do for the salary. Saw an ad for digitized flossing machines, candy-stripe vibrators for girls under ten, for do-it-yourself plastic surgery kits with celebrity templates, a handbook of enhanced interrogation techniques, robotic dogs, and plastic cats. He smiled, Reuben, or tried to, but then suddenly out of nowhere vomited violently on the floor, a commonplace mishap occurring more and more frequently these days as he remained longer and longer in California.

It was near to five in the morning, just time enough to shower and shave and trim his hair for the encroaching day. He had above $90 in his wallet, a brace for his leg, and a graduate degree.

Twenty-one

The varlet divided his summer between the laboratory and apartment, and then in August was drafted by a much-admired biotechnology company in Seattle. Interviewed three times (and having come to know only too well the quality of the recruiters), he reluctantly agreed to the position. The building was enormous, and the scientists, many of them, were dressed in blue jeans and earrings and boasted large collections of rap music. He avoided their faces and, as always, deferred speaking to them for as long as he could. So why then had he consented to join such a group in the first place?

Well, there was the sea of course, as also an opera house that concentrated on Wagner. Contenting himself with night performances only, he used to stay past midnight, reveling in the singers, his attention fixed on the stain glass roof that on clear nights admitted a sight of the stars and moon. It is true that each such performance always finally came to an end, a *coitus interruptus* that left him in a bitter mood and in no proper state to be driving home again.

On the other hand, his material situation had greatly improved. With an annual salary above $270,000, he was able to save the greater part of it, which he routinely invested in molybdenum buy options and a regularized program of short-selling the country's main art market index fund. It almost embarrassed him to find that within five months, he was "earning" more from these investments than from his already very lofty annual wage. And then, too, there were the two patents he had had to share with a colleague and his former university. True, these rarely fetched him more than $5,000 the month, a humble sum deposited automatically in a Defense Department project to recalibrate a global satellite system empowering the country's military to discontinue terrorists at long distance with positron beams. All in all, he could now rely upon nearly 20,000 Rimini *each month*, the typical cost of a basic two-bedroom home for bottom-caste people.

His own home was considerably smaller than that. Asking and receiving permission to house his book collection in a storage space next to his lab, he needed no more than seven-hundred square feet of domestic space, room enough for his stove, cot, and writing table. He had a file cabinet for his papers, including some 150 pages of last-minute suggestions from Leland and his wife. He had just three photographs: his father, the shack that person had built, and his all-time favorite dog, a brown animal with shredded ears. He had shoes—they wore out so quickly—and a few basic pieces of fishing tackle. He had other things—underwear, two sets of cuff links, 325 gallons of distilled water, a rebuilt short-wave radio, and two functioning computers attached wirelessly to the progress of his on-going experiments.

He never went to work unless he wanted to. Sometimes his mood was for reading, sometimes the sea, occasionally for the eastern mountains visible from his window. He had an arrangement with a nearby stable (his sole luxury) for a blooded stallion who could carry him fifteen miles from the city and bring him back again. Of cigarettes, he "constructed" them (as novelist William Gay used to say) himself. He liked to smoke them in the most unlikely places, despairing that ever he would find anyone willing to challenge him the right. He granted himself one daiquiri each day, his favorite beverage apart from well water extracted out of the cold hard ground.

Seven months on the job and the promise of yet another patent, he turned twenty-eight. Came April, he began looking in his lackadaisical fashion for a woman, by preference a forty- or perhaps forty-five-year-old whose history of promiscuity did not run to extremes. A widow mayhap, or mother whose children had grown up and gone away, or perchance a divorcée who indulged in poetry or painting—(he laughed)—or something of that kind. Instead he was directed to a thirty-eight-year-old statistician in the next building who, according to his colleagues, had expressed an interest in him.

At first, he offered her concerts and expensive restaurants, and when that failed to ignite her, escorted her to a rock concert that twice sent him reeling off to the men's room. The music was ludicrous, and the youths on stage had long since crossed over to the subhuman stage. He reached for his revolver. And yet on second thought, he saw nothing in that whole vast auditorium that couldn't have been corrected by twenty or thirty years of hard labor in southern fields.

Displeased by his living quarters, she tossed her jacket on the desk (disturbing the pens and pencils there) and then began consuming rather too rapidly his special concoction of rum and vermouth. Reuben stood by, making no objection when she plucked one or two books from his cabinet and looked them over without much interest. Her hair was black and her eye make-up like Cleopatra's. Moving to the other side, he viewed her breasts, confirming that for this occasion at least she was doing without brassiere. Buttocks? He put them at about a six on his personal ten-scale, though really he would have preferred a somewhat more conspicuous exhibition in that area.

He offered a spate of kissing and whispering and finally undressed her just after 11:45 and jumped on top. Not that he could expect any very lengthy proceeding! Not after three full years of a celibacy that was only partly voluntary. They were disappointed, both of them, although he intended to make up for it after a sort of intermission, which followed "hard-upon." He had never in his whole life been able to shut off his mind completely, and now found himself thinking more seriously about this ungainly thing they were doing. The woman was nothing but a composite of blood, bone, piss, lymph, and shit. This one moreover wore a dead expression that permitted him to see deeply into her opened mouth and find six silver fillings in there and a tiny excrescence on her sandpaper tongue. He *might* have been able to go on with it; instead he halted of a sudden, dismounted, and drew off into the bathroom where he vomited as quietly as possible.

They spoke briefly—she was tolerant and forgiving and much more appealing to him in her clothes. He complimented her at length, took all the blame upon himself, mixed another drink, and paid for the taxi out of his own pocket. So thus Reuben, who at age twenty-eight *never sought for any more of the same* and forever absolved himself of one of life's main problems.

Twenty-two

After a certain time, those with revolutionary potential will naturally begin to recognize each other. They might be in meetings, or collide into each other on message boards, or they might be called to one another's attention by personality archetypes exposed on holographic actualizations. Even Reuben, most unsociable of all beings, even he began to see there were others in the Corporation (and in the world at large), who lacked only the tutelage of Leland to have ascended to his own measure.

For example, there was a bald man with bright eyes who already had approached Reuben on more than one occasion. Not part of Reuben's research team properly speaking, the two of them had met up in a tavern where the varlet was sometimes wont to tarry in order to study the slobs moving in and out, fools with weak brains and strong opinions.

"Oh, yes!" the man had said. "I know *your* type. But first of all, may I buy you a drink?"

Reuben permitted it. The man was not a queer—the
boy was pretty sure of that—and moreover he was accompanied by three books whereon he was balancing his mug
of beer. Without revealing any excessive curiosity, Reuben
detected that one at least of those volumes was a bruised
copy of Fabré's *Tribulations* . . . The man went on:

"And so you come in here to get out of the sun. Me,
too. So, what's the story with you after all? Autism? I knew
it had to be something like that."

Reuben denied it. The man went on:

"OK, you don't have to say. But look here, these people
in here" —he indicated about at the trash that filled the
place— *"they'd tear you to pieces,* if you weren't as large as
you clearly are. And didn't have that big ole gun in your
pocket."

Reuben's drink was satisfactory, as also the glass of water with which to wash it down. All his life the child had
wanted his ice to be of a certain size, larger than an acorn
but smaller than a lemon, and as nearly transparent as
science could make it. For in this way it chimed more
cheerfully when the little aggregates brushed up against
each other. Running his gaze to the end of the bar and
back, he then identified at least three persons who despised the very sight of him. But would ever they *do* anything about it? Not in a thousand years.

"Not a real good fit for you, is it? Seattle? No, nor any
other place either.

And since they can't change *you,* you wish to do it to
them. See? I told you I knew your type."

Not much question but that the fellow was insane,
judging by his fluttering hands and certain other indications. All the same, the child found himself listening keen-
ly to this person, who already had divined more about
Reuben than any other coastal resident up to this date. It
was then the man grabbed up a paper napkin and jotted
down his name, address, genome, and the place and date

of a meeting where Reuben could expect to be enthusias-
tically received.

He walked home, a modest distance that took him
through a Hindu region of movie theaters, jewelry stores,
and specialty shops of the sort that gave pleasure to those
with an Asian cast of mind. He almost never saw white
persons in this neighborhood, one more suggestion that
the country was in an increasingly great hurry to exit
Western civilization once and for all. He passed an exotic-
looking boutique offering overpriced merchandise designed to appeal to the hysteria that marked the town's
most advanced people. He passed a bookstore with a window full of generic rubbish and came then to his real destination, which is to say a squalid but also archaic-looking
printers' shop doing business in the old way. He saw, saw
Reuben, neither computers nor anything else save two
ink-soiled boys and an antique press (about seven feet
tall) that might have been salvaged from sixteenth-
century Venice, or some other place of that same time and
kind. He entered, the varlet, and stood about, marveling
at the confusion, the noise, and the fat man (shirtless)
who came toward him from out of the depths of the very
long but also very narrow establishment.

Impossible not to shake with the person, as jolly as he
was and thrusting forward an ink-stained hand that was as
big as the paw of a creature that in this case would have
had to be exceptionally large.

"I have your book," the man said with huge pride. "And
I'm going to let you see it, too."

Reuben followed him back to a private "office" of some
nature, a most cluttered place with sheets of manuscript
hanging on wires. Expert in gold leaf and rubricating
techniques, some of the leaves looked as if they more
properly belonged in a museum, or a trillionaire's house.
Reuben now took over into his own hands the ten (only
ten) rather plain copies on coarse brown paper of the

twenty-three sonnets, most of them in Greek, composed by him during his lax hours at the lab. Satisfied with the appearance of the thing, he took even greater pleasure in the woodcuts, some no larger than a stamp, on which he had lavished so much time and care.*

He paid (too much) for the copies and was about to exit the place when by hap his attention fell upon a fresh-made copy of Leon Rutiger's *Magick Land* bound in a plasma of some kind. At once Reuben appropriated the thing, an underestimated work out of print these hundred years. He lacked nothing now, unless it were the Baskerville *Virgil* of 1757.

Guarding the books in his left hand, he strode homeward in what for him were pretty good spirits. (His right hand remained unoccupied in case he needed his gun.) He passed through an immaculate zone of four- and five-story mansions housing the country's worst individuals. In front two young women in short skirts were jesting and laughing and looking about happily at the clear evening sky. They formed a pretty picture that Reuben could observe with objectivity, devoid of the erstwhile lust that once had interfered with the clarity of his abnormal mind. He preferred the stars, in particular two "orange runts," as they were known, currently running away from earth at three times light speed, a gait that rendered them forever invisible but for some dozen cosmologists in possession of the most up-to-date telescopes.

Reuben was not yet one of these (cosmologists) but had given thought to becoming one. He was young and his eyes were good.

Finally, just four blocks from his own apartment, he cut through a black neighborhood of that race of men who

---

* By 2061, only two copies were known to have survived. Offered at auction, the "Corinthian edition," so-called, had brought $2.1 million from an unrevealed collector.

had been treated so badly and for so long that obviously something was wrong with them. He saw a woman with a gigantic goiter, and almost too late remembered that the district was suffering from an appalling virus brought hither in a group of 700,000 Namibian immigrants needed by a chicken processing company.

When it came time to go to bed, the boy drew off into the east room where after a certain time he was mentally able to shut off the random noises that came from town. In the silence that followed, he soon lapsed off into the same metaphysical, (as he thought of it), metaphysical dream he had inherited from Lee: a pink ocean, as tenuous as atmosphere, that ran to shore and broke into billions of splinters that drained off into the sand. In other words, he imagined that he had come to the end of his earthly punishment and need now only to dip his toe in the substance in order to *join with it* and become unconscious at last. And that was the whole of that dream, except to mention the two or three individuals—tiny figures!—waving to him from coastlines of their own.

He dreamt the dream twice more and then at about 2:00 in the morning retrieved a single printed page of some controversial mathematics and carried it to bed. He had improved very significantly in this particular science, but also had begun to run up against certain biochemical expressions where not even the most venturesome equations seemed to apply. And in short, he had begun to wonder if science really had to do with reality, or whether people like himself were always looking deeper into the mistaken conceptions of their own ill-constructed minds.

Twenty-three

He was awarded his fourth patent the same day he became a millionaire, a development that incited him to still greater frugalities than before. His theory, discredited by the experts, was to focus his investments narrowly in grain futures and interrogation technology, growth areas (he believed) for the major Western economies. And so thus by age of thirty he was accustomed to earning or losing hundreds of thousands each and every year.

Corrupted by wealth, he went back to women for a brief period in 2036, before eftsoons forsaking the process for a second and final time in September of that year. Against his best interests, he began to be tempted by the study of linguistics, paleography, ethnology, and several other fields that would have interfered with his professional time. In literature he read nothing but poetry now, and nothing after 1910. The West was dead.

Spina bifida was up, and Hodgkin's Disease had crossed the 20% line. He personally was acquainted with the child of one of his colleagues who combined mongolism, Tourette's syndrome, and albinism in one person. A golden age of cretinism, followed closely by hydrocephaly, congenital schizophrenia, and other concomitants of final decadence. It was as if viruses and bacteria had found the specific weaknesses of a people given over heart and soul to *equality*, most fatal of social diseases. Or rather it were the worst people who now were deemed the best, as testified by newspapers and television. He mentions here the woman who had released a tape showing her conjugating with a horse, the result of which she became the second most popular talk show host in the land. Children of both sexes were getting pregnant at the age of nine. Medicines that were effective elsewhere were obsolete in America.

Continuing in that vein, 12% were born with drug additions, leaving room for another 32% to acquire the habit later on. Fifty-eight percent had just one admitted parent, and 19% had none. He knew, of course, did Reuben, that it were a mistake to insert factual matter into a piece of fiction, but in emergency situations was willing to tolerate it anyway. No longer a country with an economy, the United

States had become an economy with a vestigial country running along behind. Sixteen percent were transgendered, and together with Hispanics, Negroes, Jews, feminists, and lapsed Aryans comprised an impervious voting bloc that varied between 60 and 70%. The nation had thus reached the very apex of its nadir when in October that year the boy was requested by his employer to attend a conference in San Francisco, a high-prestige affair having to do with an aspect of cell biology that none of his biographers has yet pretended to understand. He agreed to it, Reuben, in spite of the locale, and was in stage of lubricating his seventeen-year-old car—(he refused absolutely to use public conveyances of any kind, not since he had found himself on board a bus squeezed amongst a crowd of vociferating urbanites)—lubricating that car—(refused likewise to sleep on alien mattresses where others had been copulating, or scratching, or had gone to bed without a bath, or use a mirror that had been used by others, or sit within three seats of someone in a theater)—when he remembered the time and place of still another meeting that had been recommended him during an encounter with a mad person in his favorite tavern.

The most fateful coincidence of the twenty-first century (as it was called later on), when Reuben, clothed in a light blue suit with a poppy in his lapel, entered the ballroom of The Plantagenet Golfing Association of San Francisco and directed himself to the temporary bar set up in the center of the room. The room was dark and large and had a chandelier formed (it seemed) of purple amethysts the size of fruit. On stage a string quartet had just finished, it appeared, and the cellist and violinists were carefully putting away their tools.

He asked for a daiquiri and was served promptly by an elderly Negro exemplifying the sort of subservient manner that Reuben liked to see in these people. The drink, too, was good, although tinged somewhat with something or another he couldn't right away name. But mostly it were the people, some thirty or more middle-aged white men in suits. They were shy, or maybe just formal, or perhaps didn't know one another terribly well. The varlet stood among them, working on his drink. There appeared to be some pretty good artwork on the timbered wall, wherefore he wandered in that direction and examined the stuff.

"Mr. Pefley?"

Reuben turned.

"*Reuben* Pefley?"

Reuben admitted that he was.

"Well now, we're certainly glad to see you here! Weren't sure you were coming."

Reuben didn't immediately speak. The man, of middling height, was of perhaps forty years and well enough dressed, although missing one arm. To shake with him Reuben had to take the fellow's left hand.

"Molecular biology, yes? No! I don't mean that's the *only* reason we wanted you here."

Across the way a woman in an evening gown had entered the room and then, finding that she was among serious people, turned and went out again. Meanwhile two young boys, Negroes also, were setting up an array of folding chairs, a noisy procedure that discouraged Reuben from speaking any further.

He chose, the monster, a place near the rear of the crowd where he could watch these people and evaluate them one by one. One person, largely bald, held an open ledger in his lap while just next to him an elderly sort of man was gazing down sadly at the floor. He saw, saw Reuben, just one or two persons of about his own age, and even they were older than him. This much was certain, that not a man among them could have represented the slightest danger (in the physical sense) to his own person. This however was a realization so familiar to him that Reuben no longer thought about it very much.

Two minutes went past, the men whispering to one another, or snuffing out their cigarettes, or peeping into the agenda distributed by the boys. Of the names (names listed neatly in the margin of the page) Reuben knew only his own and that of a notorious journalist lately released from a two-year sentence for latent racism. To make himself the only one still smoking, Reuben now ignited one of his Syrian cigarettes, a seven-inch article with powerful tobacco. But no one offered to notice.

The speaker was a self-effacing sort of person who had been drafted against his wishes to open the meeting. Bending forward to pick up the man's almost inaudible words, Reuben began to learn about this meeting's purpose (to turn the world around) and the strategy the group had assigned itself. He now began to hear things he had not heard before, specifically that while the democracy was as yet too entrenched and too popular by much, yet there might be other ways to bring about the victory of quality over quantity and turn the world about.

His excitement increased when the second speaker brought forth a cart loaded with novels, most of them by women, and regaled the crowd by reading aloud random paragraphs from each and every book. Impossible not to laugh, even among a crowd as dour as this one. It was as if the authors had composed their "prose" while lying in warm bathwaters, or perhaps they hated English, or rather it was as if informality had reached a level that simply couldn't be carried any farther. (His mind, Reuben's, wandered back to eighteenth- and nineteenth-century times.) From there the speaker moved on to prize-winning authors, American and British, whereupon the laughter and the hooting brought his time at the podium to an end.

The following speaker had brought this morning's *New York Times* and was trying to add up the trillions that would have to be spent, the editor said, to bring people more in line with each other. As it happened, the paper had more than forty pages, providing one (and sometimes two) souvenirs for every member of the crowd.

Reuben had wished for the editorials but ended up with the music review, a cluttered sheet carrying the photograph of a new rock group of transgendered clones. He looked at the lyrics, Reuben, but found so many newly-minted obscenities that he couldn't get the gist of what exactly the group wanted to do to the guitarist's mother. For future reference, Reuben grabbed for his pencil, and marked down the names of the band members, and the reviewer's, too. "Nothing here, gentlemen," the speaker said, "that couldn't be resolved by twenty or thirty years of hard labor in southern fields."

Twenty-four

He came back from San Francisco with seventeen names and coded addresses, and right away set up a correspondence with all of them. Communicating by code, he learned the group disposed collectively of above a billion-and-a-half Rimini, a relatively moderate sum for a modern organization, but enough certainly for the beginning of propagandistic efforts. In a nation controlled by television, the group sought a station of its own capable of competing in terms of ignorance and vulgarity with the existing ones. They sought a newspaper, sought also to buy a certain Federal representative who was ready, he said, to turn his back on Ashkenazi money. They sought speakers and performers, pornography studios, a meth monopoly, a basketball franchise, and hoped to take over an extraordinarily profitable civil rights charity with branches in several countries. As for the new member, they asked only for $100,000 as a pledge of faith.

In the event, he sent twice that amount and asked for and was given a position on the Science and Culture Committee. Always he had been a hard-working type, ever since Lee, but now he began in truth to accelerate his work on a new vaccine that might actually harvest the sort of funds that would be needed. His investments that up until this time had produced only the most trivial profits, were beginning to yield 20 and 30%, and in one case had given him a $400,000 yield against a $70,000 bet on testosterone futures. And then, finally, in January he demanded a 50% salary/royalty increase that was duly granted. (Not that his team leader would have dared do otherwise.)

The next three months in the life of the whelp appear to have been uneventful, apart from a brief trip back to Alabama where he joined an exploration of the Devonian volcano field that supplied the state with much of its tourism income. Departing from the main group, he scrambled to the summit of one of the larger cones, an aesthetic experience that summoned memories of the life and times of Empedocles, strange man whom Reuben ranked among the best of the Greeks. Leaving Poludia, he drove on down into the waning foothills of the Appalachian chain where once his people had tried to get a living out of a few dairy cows and sale of arthritis remedies. The house, or shack really, was still there, as also a few shards of a painted churn and a grindstone without a treadle. Looking back upon it from this distance, it seemed beyond belief to him that at one time the country had *not* been decadent, and that he himself had actually been in existence for a few months during that period.

He proceeded thence to Lee's place, previously a three-story structure turned into a sales outlet for state and federal lottery tickets. Here he dawdled briefly, remembering Leland's lectures and punishments, his garrulity and ability to awaken fear in the boy, the last person ever to do so. The barn was gone of course, as also the stone "chair" at the edge of the valley where Lee would sometimes deposit himself for a six-hour session of hard thinking. Gone, too, the creamery, and Judy's rather poorly organized garden that had helped to feed them through the fragile times. He daren't, dared not Reuben, to possess himself of Leland's "chair," a measure of respect for the man who had behested him to his present estate. "Ah, and so *that's* why I speak so seldom," the boy went on. "I sound too much like him."

He returned to Washington (State) at the end of February and in the midst of other duties began to take a better share in the activities of the "Station," as the group of reactionaries termed itself. He had little trouble in recruiting a former friend of his, a retired roulette savant from Pskov who detested post-modernity as much, almost, as Reuben. The man was above eighty years in age and had little hesitation in turning his estate over to the group, a generous donation totaling above eighteen million dollars and a seventy-room retreat in the Canadian Rockies. Two months later (after the physicist had attended another meeting), he handed over the money right away instead of requiring the association to wait for it.

Reuben's second (and much more stubborn), recruit was a tall, lanky, red-headed automobile mechanic from Calera who in his younger days had slain two persons in a hideous knife fight eventuating in an annual stage production that continued to draw visitors from three surrounding states. It needed Reuben two trips back to Alabama and a cash reward to wheedle the fellow to Washington (State) and then set him up in a deteriorated hotel among derelicts of his own classification. He hadn't, Reuben, been a member of The Station for more than ninety days, and already he had swelled its membership by two. Followed then a period during which the boy disappears from the surviving records, reemerging six weeks later as Head of Research with a gene manufactory in the town of Lavrentiville in Massachusetts. Certainly, he hated to abandon Seattle's high-grade opera house, not to mention the

Walpurgis Inn, where he had earned the privilege of being left alone when on his homeward treks he used to enter the place to rest his damaged leg. Hated to leave the cold Pacific and hated most of all to find himself lodged among the most repugnant people in the country.

And yet . . . Truth was, he could not refuse a 20% ownership in this company and must perforce suspend the lofty disregard that had become his habit in connection with other offers. A 20% stock position, 25,000 warrants, three months of sabbatical leave, and a woman (he refused her) who had been selected in conformity with popular tastes—it was too much to ignore. Nor could he be oblivious to the Widener Library, despite its clientele. Nor the Peabody Museum, nor several other things as well.

Really, how could these people been foolish enough to hire their future worst enemy? His "superior," who possessed 53% of the institution, was an orgulous fool of the northeastern type, a credentialed but gaseous personality full of hair implants. Reuben quickly added his name to the roll call being compiled by The Station, a list of the most odious people then dwelling in the lower fifty states. Unfortunately for this person, he had a daughter of twenty-two years, an unlovely maiden who had needed less than a minute to fall forever in love with the villain. Reuben took out his ever-improving charm and used it on her.

"We're so lucky to have you!" she submitted. And then: "I've seen your bio."

The boy sloughed it off and then used his free right hand to set back in place one of her curls that had gone awry. That did it. She blushed, her juices flowed, and her orifice began to dilate.

There were other people at that party, not to exclude a government man in a green gilet, a queer who had something to do with regulatory enforcements pertaining to something or another. Reuben stood back and then shook loose one of his own curls that was wont to fall romantically across his forehead. He could have crushed the man's skull in his unassisted right paw. Came next his superior's wife, a withered person—Reuben rather liked her—who had never wanted to be here in the first place. And yet his Will hadn't yet developed far enough to transpose her by thought alone back to her kitchen, her sitting room, or wheresoever it was she wished to be.

Finally, he was introduced to a clutch of lab assistants, a jubilant bunch, most of them young, very excited (they said) to serve under Reuben. One had a face that was semi-intelligent. He divined, Reuben, that he could have murdered the whole lot of them with his ball-point pen alone. He was to be in control of their salaries and therefore, in America, in control of their souls. He shook all around, casting a threatening look at the assistants, a romantic glance at the daughter, and a cordial smile for his boss. He couldn't understand how that man owned more of the company than did he.

He never got drunk, Reuben, not when he was among humans. Someday they would turn upon him—he knew it—and cut off his arms and legs should ever he let himself be intoxicated or in a weakened condition. Lately he had become able to bench press his own considerable weight and continued to carry a .357 magnum S&W weapon with chambers for eight irradiated titanium-tipped shells. His greatest strength of all? Lack of friends. And if he had given two million of his own money to The Station, still he had more than twice that sum in some rather unorthodox investments. His health was good, and if he wanted them, he could feasibly expect as many as another fifty years of self-improvement. And finally, he understood that someday his eroded leg must inevitably snap in two. It was a problem and the source of his one single weakness.

In May he traveled back to Seattle for three performances of *Parsifal* to be given on alternate nights. Later on, he was to remember the ambience of the place, and the audience that incorporated some of America's last viable human beings. It was a perilous time for young Reuben, who thus put himself in danger of emoting out loud and calling attention to himself during the opera's last measures. Even so, the musicians were *very* good, wherefore Reuben at once added their names to that other list (list of redeemable people) that had some hundred names already.

What is beauty? Vacuoles in the substrate of reality, as Schopenhauer had mooted? Not entirely, said Reuben, who thought of it as the one connection to transcendence that humans are allowed. Suddenly he hushed, embarrassed that he had annoyed the good people sitting at his side.

He wanted a crystalline civilization in which shallowness were an actionable offense, a society that makes demands upon people and where beauty was to be pursued *at any cost you'd care to name.* Wanted a delimited country with impenetrable tariffs, a lower standard of living, more modest homes, shorter working hours. A high culture (he went on), all white, with intimidating laws and a trajectory all its own. He wanted other things as well, but especially he yearned for a genius/leader who in the fullness of time would prove to be as wise and brilliant as himself.

Still muttering, he walked back slowly to his hotel, offering himself, as it were, to the trash that might be tempted to assail him and take his cash away.

He entered a bar and after estimating the quality of the Massachusettsians, opened his wallet and exposed the three or four thousand dollars that he carried always, brightly-colored bills with the portraits of rock singers on them. No one met his challenge, not even when he took out his revolver and set it on the piano where he'd never be able to get to it in time.

The night was warm, and the women had come out in droves to show off their persons. Unable to ignore printed material, he entered a newsstand and wasted a minute trying to find something of merit among the sludge of pornography and motorcycle magazines. He did buy a newspaper (a mistake) and paid for it with two pieces of plastic change. Most of the businesses were closed, save for a government office giving out antidotes to the anti-heroin tablets that had addicted half the nation. He saw a woman who, very obviously, had been implanted with one of the new vibrators. Saw people who looked like baboons. Saw a child slurping on the snot that rilled her upper lip. The town's library had been turned into a coffee shop. Saw a white male struggling to get out of the path of a Negress too slovenly fully to lift her feet off the ground. He walked through the midst of half-a-dozen youths, the only people he had so far met who seemed even half-willing to take him on. He checked for his revolver, finding that he had indeed returned it to its place.

He had wanted an inexpensive hotel, hoping in that way to avoid wasting funds that could more usefully be given to The Station. But even here, here on Fifteenth and Bob Dylan, even the ordinary-looking places had bars and gymnasiums and little shops offering art objects for sale. Not wishing to go immediately to his room, which gave a view of the city, he settled in the lobby with his cigarettes and newspaper. The room held an elderly man in pigtails and earrings, an adolescent in an obscene T-shirt, and a three-hundred-pound woman drawing circles in the air. His attention was drawn involuntarily to the television analyzing the virtues and defects of a certain supermodel's innovative evening dress. Reuben waited with growing impatience for someone to demand that he extinguish his cigarette, and when nothing of that sort was granted him, trod slowly to his fifth-story room. Not in years had the boy allowed himself to go on board an elevator, or not in northern cities at any rate.

Was he expected to sleep in a bed that had been used by others? Working quickly, he turned the mattress upside down and covered it with newspaper. His attention fell upon an article that was to prove of the greatest interest to him, which is to say the story of a nine-year-old white girl (her photo was appended) who'd been raped and killed by a Salvadoran immigrant. Twice he read the article through to the end, confirming that the killer had been given a suspended sentence by grace of a Jewish lawyer playing to a jury of northeastern men.

Twenty-five

He would not have thought that anything could interfere with this third and final performance of *Parsifal*. Wrong. Sitting in his place between two good people, his mind in spite of everything kept reverting back to the newspaper, the child, but especially the lawyer. He belonged, that man, to a highly effective crowd that already had manipulated the white majority down to nearly nothing while expecting, one must suppose, to be treated better by incoming Latin Americans. Finally, he left the theater altogether, drifted back to his hotel, demanded fresh sheets, and then began exploring the phone directory for the lawyer's information.

Morning found the boy still sitting fully clothed on the edge of the bed, a sight that must have been puzzling to the people behind the CCTV camera disguised as an overhead lamp. Ought he, he wondered, go to the man's home, or were it better to visit his office where others of the same kind were no doubt passing large-denomination bills back and forth? For twenty minutes he dithered with his gun until at last, confessing to himself that death by gunshot wound was but a trivial experience, he secreted the item among his shirts. And then he napped, a refreshing exercise carried out while still sitting erect on the edge of the bed.

The counselor carried out his business in a noble-looking building that was narrow but tall and had a golden crest above the heavy door. Reuben climbed to the appropriate floor, in this case the fourth, and inveigled his way past the receptionist, a pleasant woman whose default position was a sympathetic smile. It always awed him, the ability of women to put on smiles, a procedure that required him twenty minutes at least, and even then he couldn't do it. Next came the two secretaries, of whom one was fairly pleasant, the other much less so. Speaking in his calm, far-away, indeed legal-sounding voice, the boy then explained how it was that his son (!) had been horribly injured in someone's private swimming pool and was lying unconscious in a hospital bed. That pool, Reuben went on, had lacked any sort of protective fence to ward off little boys and belonged furthermore to a wealthy, very wealthy family that was ripe for court action amounting to millions. Her ears pricked up and her eyes began to shine. However, Reuben continued, he thought it best for his lawyer, if he could find one, to drive out to the place with a camera, before the owner could make sudden improvements, etc., etc., that might impede the suit, and so forth.

He was conducted right away into an office as big almost as a somewhat less than normal size barn. The man himself was not especially large, however. On the contrary he was short. They shook, the lawyer actually coming to his feet and greeting Reuben in a way that would have embarrassed people capable of that emotion. He had a diamond on his tie, a ruby on his finger, and both his lips were blue.

"Let's start from the beginning," the man said. "Or perhaps we don't have time for that?"

Reuben described the situation, never failing to point out that the family, a real one that Reuben had researched in the most recent *Who's Who*, were immigrants from an unpopular country and had any number of homes both here and on foreign soil.

"Arabs you say?"

Reuben admitted it.

"And the boy—he won't actually *die* from this will he?"

He might.

Dashing to Reuben's ancient car, they drove at top speed down Martin Luther King (Jr.) Avenue before turning off onto MLK, a lightly travelled thoroughfare that led out of town. Looking straight ahead, each with his own defining facial expression, they sped past the very hospital wherein Reuben's son lay dying. Except for that, there was nothing in that car except for the two men, the two men and a shovel in the bay, a shovel and a coat hanger, a coat hanger and a pair of pliers, pair of pliers and a mint-new blowtorch weighing six or seven pounds.

Twenty-six

Cheered by recent happenings, the varlet possessed himself of a new suit for the twenty-seventh convocation of The Station. It was of course true that the membership in Massachusetts was rather smaller than elsewhere; even so there were at least five new people to be introduced on this somewhat celebratory night. Reuben sat just across from one of these, a eugenics specialist known to be working on race-specific sterilization drugs. The food was good, the table octagonal, and the servants dressed in little red jackets.

By this time the national organization had seven-and-half thousand "made men," as they had jocularly denominated themselves. They owned a building in Brooklyn, another in Wichita, and still another, the best of them, in an undisclosed location in New Mexico. They had 20,500 acres in the Florida panhandle owned previously by a large-scale timber company. They disposed of slightly more than five billion dollars, most of it contributed by older people able to remember a different sort of America. They controlled five U.S. Representatives and a Senator who sat on a committee of special importance to the group's ultimate aim. They employed a world-famous currency trader who had fetched them three-quarters of a billion by his sole efforts alone. And finally, with great stealth and brilliance, they had come into ownership of photographic copies of certain new weapons designs.

The group's ultimate aim, *that* was the subject of tonight's address by a veteran of several recent wars to force democratization upon the peoples of Africa, Asia, and Latin America. As a speaker, the man had an accent, but Reuben found himself charmed by his vision of a *Confederacy of the Northern Hemisphere*, a long-term project to incorporate 91% of the world's white people (and perhaps a few Japanese) into a single polity. An organization like that, the man went on, would have all the resources needed for a rational style of life (six-room houses instead of twenty-nine), while also making it unnecessary, or illegal actually, to have ought to do with the barbarian kingdoms of the south.

A standing ovation and then a half-hour intermission for drinks and conversation. He was not especially nervous, Reuben, to be giving the next address, not since he had eschewed ever being nervous over anything having to do with the human race. That was when this year's Chairman sauntered over and dared to place his hand on Reuben's shoulder.

"It's a good thing Reuben, to have you with us. We don't want to be a group simply of embittered old men. Absolutely not, no we also want as many embittered young ones as we can get."

Both men chuckled. He was a thin person, the Chairman, who on account of certain public expressions had been water boarded over a hundred times. Reuben respected the man but couldn't permit his hand to remain any longer on his (Reuben's) actual person.

"How old are you Reuben? No! let me guess. But what would Lee say if he could see you now? No, no, you needn't answer. Just this one question Reuben, that's all I have—was it Lee who taught you how to operate a blowtorch?"

Both men laughed merrily.

"And that project of yours, varlet, the one that catalyzes cell repair—we're going to need every bit of that money to have any hope of taking over the Aspinosa television network."

Reuben agreed. It was a successful network, and the only one in the country that offered football retrospectives on a nightly basis. All that was nothing however compared to what The Station had in mind.

"We'll give 'em every fetish in the book. Snuff films! Twenty hours of professional wrestling every week. You agree don't you Reuben? All the sooner to be done with this interlude in Western history and start anew?"

They drank to it, draining their glasses just as the boy was called to the podium. It was a considerable crowd including perhaps half-a-dozen uncomfortable-looking FBI agents. But was there still perhaps some red clay residue in Reuben's voice? Enough to give away his origin in the hills? He didn't care.

Twenty-seven

By November his investments had "turned the corner,"
the man said, and were beginning to bring him the sort of
proceeds that were essential for his projects. Seeing the
direction of things, he had shorted the country's last two
publishers of serious material while staying long on mental clinics. And then by February his vaccine had been approved and he began to absorb such large sums of money
that he required the help of a Danish French American
accountant who happened to be a member of The Station.
Meanwhile he continued to commute from his bleak
three-room apartment, incongruous behavior that Leland
would have approved, he believed.

He became more hopeful, so much more so that his facial features began to take on a more normal public
presentation. In March he was introduced to a sympathetic billionaire who had won both the Haitian and North
Dakota primaries before coming regretfully to find that
politics in America was all but worthless when compared
to . . .

"Television," he said. "Who controls television controls
all." And this: "The masses will believe anything, if only it
be repeated often enough by good-looking people on television." And then: "You can even persuade the members of
superior races that they are guilty by virtue of success and
must be punished." And finally: "O ye liberals! These people seem actually to believe that if a group has been treated badly over a period of years, why then the members of
that group must be very fine individuals!"

Reuben laughed.

"They adore what is weak, and dread what is strong.
But let me ask you this, my boy: you really want to buy
that television network that comes out of Chicago? You've
talked about it often enough."

They did (buy that television network), or rather a controlling interest that entailed some very heavy borrowing indeed. It left Reuben with his money mostly gone, and his millionaire and billionaire recruits reduced by as much as half their previous worths. On the other hand, the channel reached forty (soon to be sixty-two) million persons, owing to the extreme vulgarity of its entertainment and standard issue news and discussion shows. It required Reuben just more than a month to remove the egalitarian propaganda that infected the existing programming and replace it on a phased basis with crime dramas in which the good people were not always strong women of a feminist bent, or always black. He didn't know which he enjoyed more, the bafflement and puzzled faces that now began to show up in the Chicago area, or the pleasure of dismissing employees. In the first place, people were being invited to change their minds, an unpleasant requirement that tended both to infuriate and fascinate. Meantime in second place, Reuben loved to have his program managers, advanced people with earrings and humanities degrees, loved to have them stand at attention in front of his desk as he took away their salaries and sent them on their way.

Corporations hated Reuben's network but couldn't turn their backs on the reach of its advertising, by far the country's most rebarbative. Within the first year of operation, the network had absorbed sixty-three independent stations in Iowa, Minnesota, Kansas, and other western points, an expensive project that required the purchase of three federal regulators and so frightening a fourth that no payment in his case was necessary.

Reuben wasn't easily shocked, but even he was nonplussed by the returns on what was to prove the most-watched television show of the year, a sixteen-hour serial on *A Phenomenological Survey of Nonwestern Pornography*, a title that made it impossible for the Court to suppress it. He followed this with a three-month rerun of *The Three Stooges*, a classic series that soon had the population pretending they were slapping each other about the head and face and sticking their fingers in the other person's eyes. He was good, Reuben, at estimating the country's intelligence, a knack that, amazingly, brought the company out of debt within a very brief forty-two months. Henceforward it was into The Station's own coffers that the money flowed.

By April the organizational structure of The Station had been broken into fifty pieces, each region following the disappeared boundaries of what not so long before had been "states," so-called. Reuben, assigned to Alabama, gave much of his attention to the release of violent convicts, thus doubling the chapter's membership in the brief four months of his tenure. Came August, he was called to Kansas City and in consideration of his relative youth, height, and education was put in place to contribute to the compilation of "The Settlement," as the new organic law was to be called. An eclectic instrument, it drew upon the experience of the British, the Spartan, and the Sassanian constitutions, and was designed to foster genius and excellence as opposed to simple happiness, an impossible and unworthy ambition.

By this time Reuben's reputation had enormously increased, and by age of thirty-eight already he was being mooted for a seat on the "Asterisk Council," a nine-man committee titled after the shape of the table. He still drew a salary, but in every other way had turned away from science. The country had 400,000,000 people in it, poor-quality individuals groaning under an inquinate aristocracy of rock singers, stock manipulators, and basketball players. Reuben began to think more and more about the land in which Leland once had dwelled—150,000,000, most of them overwhelmingly white. Nagged by nostalgia for a place he'd never seen, he began to have journalists,

New Yorkers, and others of that kind brought to him in late afternoon to serve as "sparring partners," as his more euphemistic biographers liked to claim.

Thursday, he showered, cut his own hair, lotioned his wound, and set out in his primitive automobile for the nearest cinema. For nostalgia's sake, he ordered a bag of popcorn, but then turned and left without paying when the hermaphrodite behind the counter cited the price. The film itself had been chosen, or rather not chosen, at random, no consideration being given to the world-famous actor and pederast who had worked as a celebrity hairstylist prior to his career in the theater. Reuben had taken a seat near the back, but then had to rise and go quite elsewhere when two youths took up in the row just behind him. The film itself, much lauded by the New York Times, had to do with a lesbian spy with big breasts involved in nuclear blackmail with a Latin American country whose right-wing prime minister was shown raping in detail the lesbian's nine-year-old crippled sister. A bold, frank, courageous, and boundary expanding production, the picture had three fuck scenes, two of them featuring full penetration. They were doing well, Hollywood people intent on undermining the middle classes. They could not know of course that Reuben was keeping a list.

He drove toward home, passing over a turbid river in which some five or six hundred bold, frank, and boundary expanding Hindus were going through their rituals. In town he saw four large and one small Chinese standing on the corner, 12,000 miles from home. The sight sickened him, causing him to throw some music on the machine. He slowed for a band of white flagellants with tambourines and begging bowls, slowing even further as he broke into a neighborhood of half-billion-dollar houses holding the country's worst people.

Twenty-eight

His power increased, his patience declined, and by the age of forty his anger left no time for science or literature or walking his big black dog. These days he summoned his guests in fours and fives, using his favorite chauffer to fetch them to his tiny apartments in Montgomery, Kansas City, Philadelphia, and half-a-dozen other places east and west. His allowance also had increased, and nowadays he was able to employ chefs and pastry makers in each several city cited just above.

It is quite true that by this time the usual opportunists had begun to pay serious attention to The Station. This is not to say that they were ready to commit to it—far from it!—not so long as the main parties and their incumbents were "lying in the weeds" in hopes of pouncing on the group when the group was least aware. But it was too late for that. With a million-and-a-half admitted members and that many more who remained anonymous, not to mention two cabinet officers and about a thousand agents assigned to foreign places, including also a collection of artists, nuclear scientists, psephology experts, and important inroads in the pharmacology profession, all that together with some 100,000 gun "collectors" had made it quite impossible to hinder The Station and frighten away its membership.

With power came privileges, and it was these particularly that appealed to young Reuben. In his third year as Treasurer, a rich time during which he had added more than six hundred and seventy-five billion to the national purse, he personally discontinued no fewer than seven individuals with his own bare fists. Compassionate by nature, he bestowed on them just one sharp pain lasting only seconds, followed by billions of years of perfect comfortableness. But that was altogether inconsequential compared to the work of *Tom Collins* (a pseudonym) the shadow Secretary of Police. No one knew the size of *that* one's achievement.

Things now began to fall together, bringing control of oil and gas supplies. It were far easier, Reuben noted, to cause a population of 400,000,000 to misconstrue where power resided than for a man to hoodwink his own spouse. As for the people, they believed that the old constitution still held sway, that elected officials not only presided but also decided, and that the best use of a mind was to hold 90% of it in reserve at all times. Assigned to this last-mentioned problem, Reuben sketched out a reform plan that later on was accepted in principle by a six-to-three vote in the Asterisk Council.

First, he had his accountants add up the funds that had traditionally been squandered on uneducable people, a terrifying sum matched only by remittances to Israel. (Not that the boy imagined he could do anything about Israel, not for as long as New York remained what it was.) Following that, he computed the cost of humanistic studies that had been foisted upon people who would naturally have preferred to be mechanics, plumbers, waitresses, college professors, truck drivers, or software people. For him, nothing could be more dispiriting than to come across such types in the military, or in governance (as then understood), or as placeholders where decisions had to be made.

Thus his proposal to offer just four years of tax-paid education, enough to train an average person to inscribe his own name, do basic ciphering, and turn on a television set. It was a policy that was to save above a trillion-and-a-half dollars over the course of the next two fiscal years, money that was to be diverted, if Reuben had his way (as eventually he did), to the construction of three Italian opera houses with stain glass windows. He asked for a dozen five-hundred-man submarines, a radio telescope for Nebraska, a hundred recruiters posted to European uni-

versities, and a 20,000,000-volume retrospective library
designed to collect and publish in all living, dead, and dying languages. And even then there was left over money,
enough to set up a charm school for the sort of girls that
up until this time were fated to become whores or stage
performers and the like.

His real interest of course lay in the higher forms of
education, a personal specialty of his based upon his time
with Leland. He realized quickly that the country had
twelve times more schools and universities than students
qualified to use them. Accordingly, he sold the majority of
them to productive enterprises, a much-criticized action
that nevertheless brought him better than 500,000,000,
not to mention the even larger sum that would cumula-
tively have been needed to maintain them. (He loved to
see the faces of tenured faculty members, an anemic breed
heretofore immunized from "life in the round," as Leland
described the situation.) Now, almost at once the country
became more cheerful, the result of young people rescued
from the sneers and curdled sophistication that came
from imagining they had acquired an education.

No, he preferred special institutions for people as special as himself, which is to say grueling regimes that required just as much in the way of stamina and will power
as in actual brains. (Truth was, he ranked *character* above
any of these, but declined to reward it, knowing as he did
the effect of wealth and recognition upon even the noblest
souls, yea including his own.)

Truth, wealth, character, and recognition, these were
the devils that wanted to make use of him. And where
now pray was Leland when that man most was needed?
Came then to his notice a sainted poet in danger of suicide, veritably a Chatterton who somehow had survived
full thirty agonizing years. This person was chosen specifically by Reuben for a two-years stay, all costs paid, on his
(Reuben's) rather stark estate (it included a cabin and not

much else) on twenty acres just a little bit west of Cape
Fillmore. Here, stranded amongst ice and sleet, a few doz-
en volumes, and Reuben's big black dog, the boy produced perhaps the best verse since Victorian times before
then doing away with himself after all.

Meanwhile Reuben's wealth just kept on getting bigger,
particularly after he had set up a corporation offering
pieces of soiled underwear worn by celebrities. These were
the funds that had allowed him to build a 100,000-acre
particle accelerator that persuaded the Europeans to give
up any further research of that kind. (He had suspected
from the start, Reuben, that smallness and largeness ran
infinitely, and that in time the scientists would run out of
names both for stars and quarks alike.) Meantime, for old
New Mexico, Reuben donated the "Gyre," so-called, a species of human whirlpool designed to shuttle legal and illegal immigrants back to native grounds. Giving employ-
ment to thousands of white Americans with clean records,
the organization had already implanted devices in more
than fourteen million trespassers, inspiring them to hurry
back to the Rio Grande and cross over it again. (No mention need here be made of the smaller organization, situ-
ated hard by, where recidivists were treated somewhat
less compassionately.)

And so it fell out in the course of time that Reuben
turned forty-two. Still only marginally corrupted by genius, money, and time, he continued occasionally to peep in
upon what science was doing, what good books were still
being writ, and a lot of other things as well. At one time
he had possessed five active patents, although three of
them had fallen into desuetude by now. Once he had been
able to sprint a mile in under seven minutes, but not so
now. He had been able to go a week without a drink, but
no longer. And once he had been capable of playing by
memory the entire French Horn parts of Mahler's *Eighth*,

but these days wouldn't even try. On the other hand, he had grown a good deal colder than he used to be, inspired more fear, acted with less compunction, and was accomplishing more than he ever did.

Twenty-nine

The government continued to go through complicated motions, people continued to vote, and yet not one person in ten thousand realized that a new world was aborning. Farmers continued to harvest, etc. It was, in other words, *an invisible revolution*, very like the one in Lincoln's time. For two hundred years the country had been ruled by money, till along came Reuben and his associates.

In May he applied formally for the Aesthetics Portfolio, but only to be temporarily and apologetically rebuffed by the interim Chairman, an executive decision that infuriated the boy. For a long time, he sulked in the back room of his Newark aedicule, until lured back out into the sun by a bald man bringing news of his appointment to another department—crimes and punishments. His petulance dissolved on the spot and blew away at once on the constant but mild early evening breeze.

Right away he established a personal presence on both the east and west American coasts, which had greatest need of him. Heretofore, the treasury had looked upon criminal behavior as an *expense*, and a heavy one at that. Not so Reuben, who believed the country's prisoners (some nineteen million at last reckoning), should yield enough profit to finance (to mention just one example), a trip (and back again) to *Hybriscus*, the galaxy's most newly discovered exo-planet. With its green atmosphere and atoms of five-hundred protons and more, Reuben was especially interested in learning more about that apparently very extraordinary place. He used to read about it in the back room of his Newark den.

First, he divided all the nation's felons into five main classes and introduced other measures designed to expand the total. In the first (and least dangerous) category he inscribed the names of the unintelligent ones, violent people who had ruined their lives in return for a stolen car, or had raped a man, or laid hands upon someone's book, or left litter along one of the protected highways. These people he drew together in an outdoor stadium and after lecturing them about the Jamestown people, their poverty and exiguous supplies, held up examples of certain old-fashioned tools and explained their usages. They had never seen a shovel, many of them, nor lifted an ax, nor planted a seed, nor dug for treasure, nor spun their own clothes. They listened with fascination, one of them actually shouting aloud: "Yo, man! Way cool. Wish I'd known about this . . . stuff."

Reuben was followed by a priest of some sort who blessed the convicts and then with a mournful expression began to usher them aboard G3i9 aircraft able each to transport as many as seven-hundred criminals with a mean average weight of 263 pounds. Reuben followed closely behind in a pursuit plane, unwilling to cheat himself of witnessing the miscreants decanted out onto one of the country's unmapped Pacific islands, an eighty-five-acre demesne covered in crabgrass and kudzu. He liked to get up close and examine their faces as one by one they were given a tax-paid "Jamestown kit" holding exactly the tools and weapons possessed by the original settlers. Especially he liked to see how they gazed about in all directions, dismayed to learn there was nothing but sea water for as far as they could see. At first, they groaned, these people, and then soon after began to howl. This was the part Reuben liked.

Not that he made any profit from this category of prisoners! To atone for that he mandated the construction of several dozen factories in small towns in the South and

West, dreary establishments devoid of television, weight rooms, digital hairdryers, or air conditioning. Here, attached to their benches, criminals of this second class were asked to assemble no less than seventeen quantum computers a week. Some of course refused and within a few days matriculated to the next higher level.

So much then for these people, young persons mostly, most of them guilty of slovenly appearance, jewelry and piercings, bad music, weak vocabularies, and other forms of behavior that had vitiated, indeed destroyed, the country's development. Reuben had no patience for them. He might, for example, have two or three of them brought to his Billings office where in polite voice he'd quiz them on American history or basic mathematics, or cause them to sing aloud from the popular music of the 1940s and '50s. The results never varied, and after a brief session he would normally kick each of their buttocks very hard and then send them off for a shave, bath, and loss of ornamentation, itself a profitable exercise that in just the first year alone brought The Station some $25,000,000 in diamonds and gold.

He wanted to kick the whole postmodern world. Restrained from that by his colleagues on the Committee, he turned his attention to the third (and much more dangerous) class of criminals, middle-aged people, some with incomes, who had elected to remain as if they were still eighteen years old. He would gather them up at rock concerts, suntan salons, topless bars, and kindred locations where they liked to consort with liberals, rock musicians and kindred filth. One case especially interested him, that of man and his boyfriend who had married a transgendered leather fetishist who in turn was accompanied all times by the five children borne by her to an indeterminate numbers of inseminators whom Reuben after great labor on the part of the Gender Bureau had managed to identify. Although he had never wished to be remembered in history as a murderer of people, it was a wish that Reuben had perforce to abandon very early in his career.

These criminals of the third class he assigned to a largish island in the Aleutians where the skies were drear and the water hovered around seventeen degrees. Anyone attempting to swim to the mainland would quickly be frozen as solid as one of those little icebergs that one sometimes sees, if not in reality, on television at any rate. With a climate like that, the settlement had no need to discourage escape; on the contrary, the administrators recommended it. But the distinguishing feature of this island was a long, warehouse sort of building, well heated and with good supplies of food, where the inmates could spend a comfortable night for each thousand bushels of corn and other grains successfully harvested during daylight hours. As for the most stubborn of them, they could sometimes be seen standing on shore gazing longingly toward Alaska. Suicide remained an option.

As to criminals of the fourth and fifth classes, Reuben opted not to describe their punishments at this time.

The following week (he was in Dubuque), he received a gift from one of his correspondents, a sagacious man who by undisclosed methods had determined that the country was now predominantly under management of The Station, all appearances to the contrary notwithstanding. Carrying the package into the back room of his three-room dwelling, the ruffian opened it most carefully, lest the thing be loaded with dynamite. Instead, he had been given some dozen cultural artifacts from a hundred years ago, music and films, books and photographs.

He had heard about this period, a time before polygendered whorehouses. It seemed to him, too, that Leland had spoken of this era, citing it as a "pretty good time," or as something that was more or less "normal," he had said. Or rather he (Lee) had mentioned it as the time just be-

fore the country had decided it didn't really wish to become another Greece, far less anything even better than
that. When the temptations of wealth and pleasure had
blown all other considerations quite away. Or to express it
in quite another way, when America decided to become a
pile of shit.

To begin, Reuben played a recording of Tony Bennett's,
followed closely by Patti Page, Billy Eckstine, and Mel
Tormé. Was it possible? That at one time the democracy
was capable of songs that were actually "pretty good"?
Putting aside the music, Reuben then hurried on to William Faulkner and read a full chapter of some of the most
mysterious prose since Dionysius the Areopagite. But
mostly it were the photographs, faded images of families
posing proudly with their dogs and cars, cheerful little
girls in patterned skirts, baseball memorabilia, and, yes,
an apple pie (fork holes in the crust) cooling on a window
sill. His mind raced back to another saying of Leland's,
namely that in those days women had no wish to be like
men.

Thirty

It was less than eighteen months later that the Chairman of the Committee fell into a coma, and Reuben was
selected to take his place on an interim basis. He wel-
comed the increase in authority, the child did, but regretted the Chairman's fate, a man he admired more than any
other. A veteran of the Bolivian, Pakistani, Italian, and
Kirghizstani wars, the man had been charged in 2017 with
latent racism and given a nine-year sentence in the same
cell with some of the nation's most vibrant people. In that
way he had become perhaps the most qualified of all
American subjects who actually knew what needed to be
done.

The burial was held *in camera* at a nearby psychedelic cemetery with only the Chairman's wife and members of the Committee present. Here, gathered under the magnolias, Reuben was invited, and consented, to take the vacant post for a period of not less than nine-and-one-half months. And so thus Reuben, who at age of forty-four had become the Western Hemisphere's most powerful personality by far. He agreed to the terms (most of them imposed by himself) and after shaking hands with his colleagues, retreated to his Nashville apartment where in order to remind himself that he was but just a human after all, had caused himself to be flagellated by the only aide willing to do so.

He liked to go downtown and walk about, bemused that no one recognized him or understood the extent to which they were already conforming to his policies. He might for example borrow a cigarette or ask the time of day, fascinating experiences that allowed him to look into the unfocused and rather hazy faces of ordinary people.

Two weeks into his new authority, Reuben called a meeting of the Aerospace and Communications Lobby, the biotechnology people, two rock stars, The Audubon Society, the hockey franchise, large scale western landowners, pornography interests, the President, Casualty Insurance, and the Petroleum Consortium. He dealt kindly with them at first, even going so far as to share several obscene jokes that they seemed genuinely to appreciate. Soon however he turned to the issue at hand, explaining in a more or less calm voice that he fully understood how it had come about that Aryans were now a minority in a country that had been built upon the brains and energy of European types. They listened of course, but then soon began to make protests on the basis of "economic necessity," they said, and "market expansion." Reuben listened, his mind mostly on the 1940s and '50s, when his own people had comprised 90%. Finally, his patience at an end, he

ran his fingers through his hair, the signal for his four secretaries to rush into the room with a bamboo tripod
whence dangled a noose of nylon thread. At first Reuben
had thought to punish the Petroleum man, but then
changed his choice over to the woman who represented
insurance interests. This person was immediately hoisted
to the noose and permitted to dangle there until her eyes
took on a funny look and she was dead. No one could
have described the facial responses of those who witnessed that process, except to say that henceforth Reuben
began to enjoy a much better cooperation from that seg-
ment.

Next, to inaugurate his promotion, Reuben emptied
the prisons and pushed the inmates out to sea in little
rubber rafts. None of those people dared ever to come
back again, not once they had seen the effects of an escrubilator upon human flesh. Reuben was satisfied to let the
President take credit for this very popular expedient, a
piece of generosity that encouraged that man once again
to imagine that he was in control of affairs. Next, he (Reuben, not the President) organized the construction of a
hundred-mile pipeline that ran above ground and had
enough circumference to admit four ordinary-grade human beings marching four abreast. Reuben's project was
to export all who had entered the country since Johnson's
immigration bill of 1965 and by means of inducements
and threats, introduce them to Jalisco and other southern
parts.

Later on, inasmuch as the policy had had the extra
benefit of reducing the economy down to a more sustain-
able and wholesome size, he was to consider it the best of
his achievements. He had fallen to earth into a polity of
some 375,000,000 supernumeraries alongside perhaps
25,000,000 actual souls, and after just two years on the job
had contrived to bring the population down to 311,347,028
with two hundred million still to go. Like his mentor, he

wanted a small country getting smaller, fine people getting finer, a crystalline civilization of earnest people never
so far from libraries and opera houses that they couldn't
walk.

On the seventh month he rested, and then in October
wrought himself an invitation to Jalisco where he spent
two entire days watching people emerge one abreast into
the bright golden sun, a never-to-be-forgotten experience
preserved on film in numerous public and university libraries in the Midwest and South.

Having disposed of a great part of the country's immigrants and criminals, Reuben next turned his attention to
the some sixty million African Negroes, a lapsed population sustained on the naïveté of the authentic population.
Some lived in cities, and some did not. Some went willing-
ly into The Pipeline, and some did not. Meantime his
agents had unearthed large numbers of feminists, New
York lawyers, and billionaires whom he admitted on a daily basis to The Pipeline. Mixed with that group were several hundred necrophiliacs, twenty-eight cannibals, and
still another individual whose proclivities lay outside the
reach of a standard dictionary. The country was getting
better by the day, Jalisco worse.

His powers increased. With Christmas near, he purified
the armed forces of women, letting them off with light
sentences. Europe feared him. It was said he could have
transmuted all the wines of France into boric acid and
never hear a complaint. This was the same month he demanded (and received) a full retrospective refund from
Tel Aviv while also enduring three assassination attempts,
one by land, one by sea, and yet another in which he was
at last justified in exfiltrating his .357 and allowing it to
bark out loud and clear.

Some of his ideas came, not from Lee, but Grecian literature. He saw how Alexander's veterans had been

formed into an elite corps* of men of more than seventy
years of age, the most terrifying army then current. They
had so little to lose, don't you see. Their wives were dead
or ugly, and their children had grown up and gone away.
Trained to a sharp point, able to run only just slightly
slower than Achilles, nauseated by luxury, good with
sword and shield, etc., they took joy in defending the
world from youth's ever-recurring insolence.

He needed only a brief time, needed Reuben, to instantiate the system in America. Mothers didn't object,
whileas for the old people, they found it far better than
golf to be marching forward through woods and field
while singing songs of death.

Thirty-one

In April he returned to the Great Smoky Mountain
chain and, followed at a distance by his guard, hiked for
about forty-three miles over the course of two-and-a-half
days, until his leg began seriously to bother him. All his
life he had preferred landscapes to people and had long
ago realized that he could draw nearer to transcendence
by aid of rocks, sky, and trees than from any number of his
own abnormal species—sapiens in shoes and hats.

He wanted solitude; instead his councilors caught up
with him just as he had reached the 6,000-foot level of Mt.
Cassiopeia. In his absence, the people (he was told) were
returning to their default positions of mediocrity and
worse, and stood in need of more dreadful punishments
than any he had so far designed. Meantime three new
neuroses had broken out in California, and although the
pharmaceutical people had finally come up with a genuinely effective penile extender, they hadn't yet devised an
antidote.

---

* *The Silver Shields*

To begin, Reuben abrogated *all* federal welfare disbursements and redirected the money to postgraduate fellowships in cosmology, book binding, parapsychology, and the teaching of Byzantine Greek. Five more Wagnerian opera houses he built, all of them furnished with walls and ceilings of stain glass masterpieces "borrowed" from the states of vestigial Europe. Against the urgent recommendation of his advisers, he then relocated The New York Stock Exchange to a small town in Wyoming. This, too, damaged the economy and had the good effect of requiring millions of office thralls to walk to work instead of ride. In his imagination he seemed to see them, an etiolated population scurrying on a daily basis toward Manhattan from distant places, their good health and bright red cheeks now once again fully restored.

He liked to make his improvements two at a time. He might for example hit upon a method for reducing the economy while also minimizing contacts with non-Caucasian lands. The Northern Hemisphere provided everything except four Rare Earth Elements which Reuben was trying to synthesize in his Omaha apartment.

His councilors brought him other news, namely that some of his own people had staged a riot owing to an unfavorable conclusion to a basketball game. Three times Reuben read the message, his fury mounting by the second. His *own* people behaving like that. Hadn't he already proved that he allowed no exemptions to the new moral standards he had striven so hard to apply? White people behaving as if they were black? Taking his beer with him, he rose to his feet and walked back and forth in the *Pied Cow*, the tavern he had chosen for this consultation.

"Well, they didn't actually cause a lot of damage at least," his second-ranking advisor submitted. "Just kids after all."

Reuben looked at him. He was tired, so very tired of the "mushmelons," he called them, always recommending tenderness instead of efficacy. His desire was to hunt down these people one by one and because they were white, deliver them an even harsher punishment than was his habit. Finally, after a second beer and a good deal of argumentation, he relented somewhat and ordered simply that each rioter be identified and given a really thorough-going beating of the second degree.

He walked just six miles the following day and then on Wednesday took the swift train back to Kansas City. There was no doubt but that the people, some of them, had begun to realize who it was that hovered over the three branches of government, not to mention a good fraction of private enterprise. He caught a woman looking back at him admiringly. She was not a virgin however—far from it! —whereupon Reuben had one of his men escort her to another car. It wasn't admiration he saw in the men, but rather a sort of paralytic fear that had them all looking straight forward lest they so much as glance at him by happenstance. Would only that Lee could see their behavior, a weak people, ignorant, and far more interested in wages and possessions than in their own pathetic qualities, assuming they had even that much. Suddenly he came to his feet, all six feet and six inches of him scowling ferociously at the passengers. Which, and how many of them urinated in their trousers he couldn't accurately say. God, he loved it.

And yet he could not forget that his chairmanship was running out, or that it was still too early to demand that it be made permanent. Accordingly, he used these last weeks to exhume his benefactors Leland and the Divine Judy and with some thousand witnesses have them reinterred a few miles south of Brent in an ivory casket modeled after Abelard and Heloise's. A "closed coffin" ceremony, no one knew the lovers were embracing in that bejeweled coffin that held not only the bones of their favorite dog, but some two score of the world's best books in antproof boxes. The orchestra was a good one, as also the tenor who was in good voice that day for Mahler's *Abschied*. Afterwards, Reuben wept openly and then filled the site himself with the same shovel used two-hundred years ago for Leland's all-time favorite American person, Edgar A. Poe.

He returned in depressed spirits, hoping to ameliorate his condition by signing twenty-seven long-postponed death warrants. Tired of travel and tired of spectacle, he sent a surrogate to the executions that took place in the shade of the John Wilkes Booth monolith in Central Park. Here, to an audience of whiskey drinkers and cotton candy vendors, pickpockets, and bewildered-looking liberals, the twenty-three men and four feminists were hoisted so far up into the sky they appeared like exclamation marks, or blackbirds of reduced size, or like miscreants hoisted, as mentioned, very far up into the sky. Ended thus Reuben's nine-month tenure as western civilization's most important person.

Thirty-two

He hated to be without his chairmanship. Even so, he felt partly assuaged by releasing the Martin Luther King, Jr. orgy tapes, and then following that by demanding freedom for a certain patriotic Norwegian who had slain some ninety-six evildoers on his own authority alone. Next, he called together the country's most egregious publishers, editors, and mainstream readers, an enormous group that spilled out of his Grundy Center apartment and filled the yard. Coffee was served, also little cupcakes with icing on them. Smiling at each of his guests in turn, he then seized up one of the hundred or so best-selling novels of that day and began to read at hazard a few paragraphs of generic prose. It told, that story, about a big city woman and her troubles with men. Moving on quickly to another volume,

he quoted a full page concerning a big city woman and the
hard choice she had made to transform herself into a lesbian. The third book detailed the problems between a career woman and her old-fashioned mother. (It also con-
cerned fraught problems subsisting between the woman
and her brother.) Came next the story of an American ac-
tress and her participation in mafia operations, a bounda-
ry-pushing work that explored human sexuality in new
and daring ways. Finally, and not to neglect poetry, he
read briefly, or tried rather to read, a few stanzas of con-
vention-defying verse that had dispensed with the use of
vowels.

His face, intimidating by nature, now began to twitch.
His stomach was churning, and he had a headache. How
many of those editors and publishers, etc., how many had
not already soiled their pants? Suddenly his right arm,
which was perhaps an inch or inch-and-a-half longer than
his left, darted from his jacket and took one of the biggest
publishers by his throat. The man, a denatured New York-
er, was in possession of a neck not much thicker than
Reuben's better ankle. Squeezing and relenting, relenting
and squeezing, the child was able to put all sorts of expressions on the man's face, from that of a shriveled prune
to a bright red balloon. Relenting and squeezing, squeezing and relenting. It surprised Reuben to see two other
publishers actually rise from their chairs and attempt to
leave, ignorant of the guards just outside the door.

He saw no reason why women should be writing at all.
What, hadn't they enough to do by catering in kitchen
and bedroom to their chosen men? Could they stitch a
straight line or put up home-grown vegetables in mason
jars? And yet half these publishers were women also! That
was when one of the editors raised his hand and pointed
out very courteously that the squeezed man had lately
come out with a new edition of Thucydides with colored
maps.

Reuben dropped him. The good culture, now almost extinct, had been so eaten away, "vermiculated," he said, by awful books and music and worse television, he wasn't entirely positive that even he in his strength could restore it to life again. (His mind flitted back to the good music of Leland's youth. It flitted also to the literature of those days, the drug-free children, the fishing and dancing, the stamp collecting and girls in pastel dresses. Not that ever he had seen anything like that!)

Again, he gathered up the editor and resumed squeezing. He saw no reason why publishers need issue 100,000 execrable books each year when they could just as easily offer a dozen good ones. *Exclusion*, he said, was the principle of excellence. A polity greater than Greece always his guiding ambition. Nor could he see any decent reason for women to be sitting on corporate boards, far less to be abroad at night after the hour of nine.

He was approaching fifty years of age, and his patience was eroding. Not part of his purview properly speaking, he next turned his attention to immigration, a nauseating project that saw him rushing back and forth to the nation's boundaries. (The archives still hold a photograph of the boy squeezing a just-arrived Congolese refugee with bulging eyes.)

Finally, he turned his attention to modern art, the most entertaining of his concerns. He often went to galleries, a foolproof method for bringing him out of his despair. There, among throngs of wealthy fools, he might view a twenty-foot frieze composed in turtle blood. Or a brick lying on top of another. (He swooned at the sight.) He might (and did) examine a canvas portraying yet another canvas that had nothing on it.

Truth was, he had enriched himself enormously by investing at an early date in the work of Amadis Chen-Proudhon and his historical portraits of the backs of people's heads. Nothing (apart from celebrity underwear) had

paid better dividends to The Station, or to Reuben personally. Having summoned the man to Omaha, Reuben
kicked him three times, very hard, took his money and
contributed it to The Station.

Moving right along, he criminalized the use and production of anti-AIDS treatments, and as an adjunct to that
decision, gave out coupons for cocaine, heroin, and the
rest, hoping that people inclined in that direction might
all the sooner destroy themselves. Finally, just before he
turned fifty-one, he called a meeting of the nation's representatives at which time he tripled their salaries and announced the construction of new bridges and highways
that would bear their names. He promised to improve
their conditions and see to it that henceforward their of-
fices would contain bowling alleys, swimming pools, and
mirrored ceilings. (Himself, he neither had nor wanted
any pleasures at all; indeed, having achieved the level that
he had, the very idea of it nauseated him.) He also avowed
—and many of them believed it—that elected officials
were still in control of the important things. And finally,
before the year ran out, he required that the scoring of
intelligence tests be retargeted in such a way that *everyone
be measured on the same scale*. Nothing that he had ever
done or ever was to do ignited quite as much adversity
amongst the country's black population.

His geologists meantime had pounced upon a lake
half-hidden in the Smokey Mountain Range, a seventy-
acre body of deep blue water found to be generally free of
pharmaceutical contamination. Immediately Reuben
posted a twenty-man guard about the circumference of
that lovely place and in October personally dedicated the
site to the aesthetic needs of The Station's people. (As to
those who admired his work but later on were to assert
that he had no sense of humor, it's only fair to recall how
he paid some two million black people to adhere to the

Mosaic religion, and then transported them to the shores of Israel.)

He turned next to television, the most frightful by far of post-modernity's human destruction machines. By this time the advertisements had actually become less loathsome than the programming. But even here one could see the social engineering brought into effect by those same advanced people—billionaire Negroes served by sniveling whites, impatient female police officers barking instructions to inept males, adorable Chinese children sucking on lollipops, not to mention all sorts of other hints designed to demote the country's founding tribe. This especially made Reuben mad.

He needed two months to bring these people together, a small group of short dark people who all looked very much alike. He squeezed and kicked until his leg gave out and then, speaking in that cold voice of his, exported the whole bunch of them to The Democratic Republic of the Congo where they were free to put their egalitarian philosophy into active practice.

Money: it proved far easier to employ some of the new software than to interview these people on a one-to-one basis. Software did I say? A method for changing ownership names on stocks and bonds? Absolutely. For collecting property deeds and distributing them among The Station's people? Yes indeed.

The country was improving and the population getting thinner. By April there were three functioning Pipelines, one of them emptying out about five miles offshore in the Pacific Ocean. In March he reinstituted the traditional watermelon seed spitting contests in Alabama, and then a month later demanded an improvement in the manufacture of book bindings, of color-coordinated highways made to look like streams of gold, gamma-powered automobiles resembling Spanish galleons, flowering crabapple trees from Maine to Minnesota, radio programs in British

voices, Elizabethan clothing, timbered buildings pre-
seeded with honeysuckle vines, music by Debussy and
Ravel projected over field and dells, luminescent cattle
and magnolia trees articulate in Latin and French, mile-
high office buildings composed of amethyst, etc., etc., cus-
tom made women's faces, vacation time on the seas of the
Andromedan cluster, unification of the Greek and Gothic
pantheons. What? Yes certainly, it were preposterous at
this time to claim he did *all* these things by himself alone.

He had help. He had *Lester Plim,* a pseudonym belong-
ing to the single most merciless person of his immediate
acquaintance. He had *Rodney Sweet* (pseudonym), and
Swifty Smith (the man's real name) who between them
represented perhaps the most sophisticated engineers in
the land. He had a woman, quite old, who could see into
people's hearts, as also one *Triste Glamond,* composer of
string quartets. He had two psychics and a "magician" (for
want of a more scientific appellation) who claimed by Will
alone to force clouds to run behind the sun. He had,
enough said, *Wilmer Brittle.* He had the entire membership of a Confederate Reenactment Academy that was ever coming up with new and improved strategies of attack.
Had a fleet, had Reuben, of one-man submarines armed
with various kinds of long-range defoliants. Had *Yelena
Trude* and *Misteria* [surname deleted], espionage agents
on the job in New Zealand. He had other people, too, not
excluding the allegiance of some sixty-two million embittered white males supplied with rocks and sticks.

Had a large black dog.

Thirty-three

Later that year Reuben managed to slough off his bodyguard and go for his annual walk in Swain County in the
former North Carolina. The place was altogether large
enough for the country's very limited number of good

people, the sort who could recognize beauty when they saw it. He wanted government by these people, an austere group denied luxuries or name recognition, and from which it was easy (*extremely*) to be expelled. (One man indeed *had* been ejected already and forced by the sitting Chairman to spend the balance of his life in one of the vestigial states of Muslim Europe.)

Here Reuben stopped, his thoughts fixed upon the prospective library he planned for the best of the Americans. One could enter that library at any hour and find hundreds of his sort of people hunched over obscure volumes in odd languages, or taking coffee, or napping on red leather sofas. Here is where policy would be made, harsh laws that must be obeyed whether the populace wanted them or not.

Down below he could see a white farmhouse with a rotting barn, one of the most nostalgic he had ever seen, rotting barn with a pig posturing in the door. The country was getting poorer, no doubt about that, and with less time to indulge themselves, the people were definitely becoming less and less despicable while enduring more and more distress. Suddenly he stopped again, startled to discover he had happened upon a 270-degree view of a crowded agricultural containment center for midlevel miscreants of various sorts. He looked at them with some sadness, knowing as he did that most of these people would surely have harbored their virtues and done their homework, if only they could have seen what was to happen to them. Instead, (and here Reuben looked in a melancholy way at the clouds scuttling by), instead they were confined now for ten- and twenty-year sentences at sorghum production using Jamestown methods.

He continued on. There was no shortage in this kingdom of healthy foods certainly, not since he had put some 38% of the people, some of them free and some not, to deal with what had always been a predominant problem in pre-modern times. Good food, jeweled landscapes, observatories stationed on Betelgeuse—he felt he was at last beginning to instantiate some of Leland's preliminary demands. Meantime his physicists were making progress on the "time problem," and seemed likely to reverse the direction of that persistent illusion and even perhaps offer it over the counter in decorative bottles. So wasn't the boy entitled by now to at least some little some feeling of accomplishment? A little bit? Hadn't he earned his glass of water by taking his country in hand and turning it into the two lands known all over the world as "Peflia East" (famous for science) and "Peflia West" (famous for everything else)?

Approaching the farmhouse, he paused long enough to peer in at the window, very pleased to see there an old-fashioned radio as big almost as a refrigerator. What people were these? Books, too, he saw, as many as thirty or forty in dark bindings. And woman, a middle-aged sort of person concentrating on her sewing under a flickering lamp. The dog, too, was conservative, an unkempt creature gazing up adoringly at the seamstress. Studying the scene, Reuben could feel himself softening, his cold hard heart in danger of the sort of foolishness that could have forestalled Leland's intentions. And that, of course, was when a child (about fourteen years old) entered the room, sprawled on the floor, and began whining in a nasal voice that easily pierced the window and came to Reuben's ear immediately after. He wore a baseball cap and the tattoo of a python wrapped four times around his neck. His hair dribbled down over his eyes, he had a nose piercing, and his eyes were dead. Reuben looked at him.

Later on, in newspaper reports it was said (wrongly) that Reuben had smashed open the glass and had entered by way of the window. Truth was, he ran around to the door and, never bothering to knock, used his good foot to break the hinges. They tried to imagine the expression on those people's faces, the newspapers did. Most of all they described the son, who found himself lifted about eighteen inches off the floor.

"Hey, man! Chill!" the boy managed to utter.

But Reuben wouldn't.

Toward four in the afternoon, with his poor leg beginning to trouble him, Reuben limped into the outskirts of a village with perhaps two or three dozen private homes and a business district that occupied a short stretch of the highway. Here he paused, his enormous shadow blocking off a great part of the town. A man emerged from one of the stores, recognized Reuben, and then turned and went back in. Reuben ignored him, proceeding instead to an adorable little gift shop where some four or five female tourists were ecstaticizing over the junk on sale. One could purchase a half-pint of maple syrup in a Donald Duck jug. Or, a knee-high doll of Martin Luther King (Junior) in velvet. He rather enjoyed it when suddenly the women recognized him and left off speaking. One woman, normally red in the face, turned pale, while the others executed exactly the opposite procedure. Not one of those persons had read a serious book in twenty years. Each was carrying thousands of parasites, not to mention half-a-dozen minor diseases of which they were perfectly unaware. For a moment Reuben thought of summoning his guard and having them taken into custody, but then changed his mind when he admitted to himself that their average quality was probably no worse than about a "three," or even a "two" on the national ten-scale, and meanwhile he had many problems more pressing than them. Continuing forward, he actually doffed his cap to the next woman and made a little bow, a curious episode that made its way into more than one of the surviving records.

He limped past the City Hall, a one-room building with a corpulent policeman sitting out front in a rocking chair. He had made this, police work, the second-highest paying profession in the realm, a misdirected benevolence in the case of this particular man. He stopped, made a note in his daybook, and then plodded on to a tavern in which a score of raucous men were draining tankards of beer while listening to some very stupefying music that ought have caused the composer to be jailed. Here Reuben stopped, peered through the window, and went inside. He would have preferred not to be recognized, but it was much too late in the history of the world for that. The bartender was an especially decayed sort of person in a dampened apron. Reuben disconnected the music and in the silence that followed went and peeped into the back room where he had expected, correctly, to find a meth lab in active operation. Above the bar itself a football game was being shown on a seventeen-foot-long television screen that gave off the scent of human perspiration. He wanted to slay the lot of them. Their brains, somewhat smaller, physically speaking, than Aristotle's, were giving off a sort of white noise that seemed to come out of the empty shell of an extinct nautilus. But other than for that, no word came from the row of self-despising men all looking off in other directions. Reuben selected the worst of them and after twisting the individual's head about, stared for a considerable time into the weaker of his two weak eyes. Behind him he could hear the front door opening and closing as the remaining customers one by one excused themselves and went away.

Seldom had he seen a village as deserted as this one. A few grinning youths were clustered in front of a tavern, their bright red gums sparkling over the distance. Apparently, the people had learned that Reuben was in town. He could have slaughtered the whole lot of them and still had time left over to turn the world around.

Thirty-four

He was dawdling over waffles and coffee when a message came in over the escrubilator, a brief statement telling him that the Chairman had resigned and that he, Reuben, had been named to take the office himself. He groaned. Never as young as he used to be, he would have preferred to resign as well. His weight was ten pounds more than it should have been, while his height had given away more than an inch over the past several years. He had *not* given up on his personal perfection however, though it did require a good deal more determination than before.

He caught the fast train to Santa Fe and after taking the oath, was invested with the tiara that meant nothing to ordinary people, but everything to Committee members. A long time he had been meditating the unification of the Northern Hemisphere, and he had not held office a full week before summoning his diplomats, the relevant ambassadors, and the prime Marine Corps officers. The project he had in mind ought have been consummated two hundred years ago, an oversight that inspired the boy to indict the more important surviving decision-makers who had participated in the omission. Concerning Canada especially, he approved the demographic profile of that country, excepting only the great number of Chinese infesting British Columbia and adjacent areas.

Nothing could be easier than a country as decadent as that one. On Wednesday he made the announcement, and then the Saturday following he called the Prime Minister to his apartment in Elmira, took him into the back room, and exposed various economic and military charts that showed in plain fashion the necessary course of manifest destiny as it related to the upper shelf of northern North America. And as if that wasn't enough, Reuben had 385,000 forces parked on the unnecessary boundary that had for so long hindered the inevitable coalescence of the two states. Furthermore, there was no good reason, Reuben explained, for "Canada," so-called, to continue on forever in the cultural sterility that had distinguished the place since its earliest days.

The final announcement came on Tuesday, Reuben's lucky day. Some cheered, some despaired, some were sent to agricultural camps. As to the Chinese, their numbers at once began to thin out, a fascinating spectacle that created problems both in Hong Kong and Singapore. He didn't want them, Reuben, (want Hong Kong and Singapore) and was glad to see vacant homes made available in America's newest states. There was good timber there, fisheries, and lots of other things.

Russia, on the other hand, a more barbarous and self-respecting polity, proved contentious in the extreme. The very last Reuben now wanted was to send a couple million enfeebled self-worshipping American nitwits up against a similar number of round-headed Slavs with brass knuckles and nuclear arms. He dithered therefore, Reuben, sometimes issuing threats which he shortly followed up with well-worded apologies. By contrast with America, these people—many of them were intelligent—cared about the national genome and were profoundly disinclined to come into too close approach with a philosophy that had done such damage to the West. Nor did they wish to be absorbed into the huge country just to their immediate south. Reuben never tired of pointing to this latter threat, even going so far as to provide the leadership with an educational tour to Guangxi and back.

In August he invited the Russian President and two council members down to Texas for a five-day festival of deer hunting, barbecue, and girls. He pointed down to Mexico and the threat that he, with all his skill, had only just barely managed to advert. He pointed all the way to Honduras and further even than that. He pointed to southern Chile and, continuing on, all the way around the pole and back to China once again. Impressed, the Russians shook hands with him, slapped him on the back, drank further beer, and shot at everything in sight. *Their* genome, at least, seemed perfectly intact.

The states of Eastern Europe! In dealings with these people he needed only to point to their extraordinarily unfortunate location between round-headed people on one side and German Teutons on the other. The Poles were first, who immediately signed Reuben's proffered document and right away contributed their pathetic fleet to the unified command at Mobile. Encased in a protective shell guaranteed by Reuben, the Poles now at last began to demonstrate what they could do—raise pigs, manufacture simple furniture, and harvest German crops. As to the other states in that unfortunate location, they all capitulated soon after. All save the Serbs who managed at last to accomplish what Rueben so far hadn't—cajole Russia into joining the club.

By this time, with Reuben approaching his sixtieth year, the Northern Hemisphere was almost complete. Based upon their pig-headedness, paintings, and calligraphy, he even thought about the Japanese, but then pushed it out of mind after consulting with his geneticists. Still, he did admit approximately 2% of other peoples, if only to remind the hemispheric citizenry of what they weren't. That other hemisphere, the southern, could rot for what he cared. Oh yes, it still sometimes happened that people from that region would penetrate Reuben's *Northern Confederacy*, he called it, in search of food, clear skies, or because they wished to live in a lawful society. The greater part of them were very soon captured however and auctioned off to corn and soybean farmers in Illinois, Iowa, and certain other states. He had built, had Reuben, a golden realm that held 38%—the rest could rot—of the world's best people. Governed by non-elected officials drawn mostly from the small-town American South, the national prosperity nevertheless soon began to increase unnecessarily, and had to be curtailed by shorter working hours. He had wanted a crystalline society of naïve people living cheerfully in five-room houses, each man his dog and woman, and every child his baseball glove. (Ambition was largely useless in a society of this nature, a condition that had driven 83% of the Ashkenazim quite insane.) A land of books and agriculture, a prelapsarian world as genteel and pleasant, as romantic and consensual as 1950. A world (he went on) of dancing and fishing and evening walks instead of television, a front porch on every house, and the sound of conversation at midnight. But would he get it?

Thirty-five

He liked to spend his days in the back room of one or another of his well-located apartments. Here, scanning the reports that came to him from all parts of the Caucasian world, he saw that crime was down, while the population of the agricultural work camps was up. It was clear to him that the good people were at last benefiting from the labor of the approximately ninety-eight million who were bad. (Always there would be bad people, even in this most propitious of places.) But as to the very worst of them all, stock manipulators, rock musicians, and mainstream publishers, these he either executed with his own two hands, or exiled to the other side of the equator.

Even an hour earlier, he had been younger than he was just now. His mind, still the world's most brilliant, was slower than he liked to admit, and meanwhile he had lost the gist of the most recent advances in his chosen fields. Accordingly, on Thursday week, he ventured from his Wichita apartment and took the fast train to Montgomery. Stars were falling on Alabama, or else those were the quantum satellites recently hoisted into orbit at his command. He strode past an old-fashioned Negro, putatively blind, with a begging cup and guitar. Reuben, who loved such scenes, waited till the song was over and then donated the fellow a little silver coin.

He did not much like being abroad in daylight; even so he continued striding forward for a considerable time before colliding into a promising youth as big, almost, as himself. They looked each other up and down, Reuben remaining silent to allow the man to apologize.

"Oh!" the young man said, jumping back. "You!"

Reuben admitted that he was. Encouraged by the boy's perspicacity and the two high quality books under his arm, Reuben led him to the nearest bench, sat him down, and began then to interrogate the fellow about all sorts of matters related to the subjects they discussed. It turned out to be an interview that continued over three days, a stressful time interrupted only by the need to absorb and expel the good water offered by a nearby fountain famous in that locale. Reuben quizzed him on the books he was carrying, on theory and practice, the kind of girls he preferred, his knowledge of old-time cartoon characters, chemistry and physics, and which Wagnerian opera he most preferred. Satisfied, at least in part, Reuben sent a message to the child's parents and then threw him aboard the next fast train to Kansas where for eighteen months he suffered under the rule of some of the most learned and temperamental docents then extant. (Hard to believe that in old days the nation's leaders had actually been chosen by *election*, an embarrassing process that twice each lustrum called the general ignorance into play.) Reuben never saw him again.

He was getting old, Reuben, and he knew it, yes, and the people knew it, too. Instead of weapons and cigars, the gifts that now came to him came in the form of silk pajamas and fur-lined shoes. (Other gifts, not mentioned here, comprised homemade bombs secreted in decorated boxes, ricin cakes, and like objects that he forwarded on to *New York Times* editorial writers.)

Better still was the pleasure he took in appearing suddenly in various places and examining the improvements that he and Lee had wrought. Crime scarcely existed anymore, and almost every house he saw had a large front porch. With television curtailed to just thirty minutes a day, families had begun to eat together, a reactionary habit causing a dearth of business for divorce lawyers. No longer were Negro youths to be seen prowling white neighborhoods with their pants between their knees. No indeed, most of these were working in the fields. Girls—he was pleased to see them once again in ribbons and gingham dresses, their knees in constant contact with each other until well past eighteen.

He liked to go into mines and factories and follow yesterday's billionaires as they perspired and groaned and, very often, collapsed the moment they caught view of him. He seldom actually killed any of them however, or at least not till they had completed their ten- or twenty-year sentences. He even enjoyed going into the surviving publishing houses and sitting among workers grinding "pulp into pulp," as Reuben's successor was said to have said.

Under heavy bodyguard, he enjoyed exploring old-world cities, inhabited these days by irreconcilable urbanites still lined up in front of nightclubs, stock brokerages, handicraft collectives, and adorable little restaurants. Out of charity Reuben had even provided for weekly cocktail parties hosted by wealthy middle-aged ladies in evening dresses. *Formerly* wealthy, he should have said.

He liked to visit the headquarters of *The Washington Post*, and on one occasion had even gone so far as to shake hands with that institution's affirmative action goy, a sheepish man always looking down at the ground. More interesting yet were the universities, laminated white marble buildings staffed these days by normal-looking men. Only once did he espy an adult in pigtails and strange glasses, and after causing his driver to stop, had punished this individual with his own two hands. Things were getting better! Having demanded and received the Israeli Refund, the average American now worked just three hours the day while his wage remained 30% over and above what was essential both for basic survival and golf, gym, and tennis dues. He loved, loved Reuben, to switch on the television and confirm that nowadays the news was delivered by elderly scholars instead of haughty blonds with high-cost dimple implants. Some of those girls had been sent to the fields, while the best of them had entered decent marriages and were honoring their husbands. Satisfied with his inspection, Reuben next took the fast train to Billings and allowed himself an *aperitif* of absinth and a two-course meal, all which led in turn to nine full hours of high-grade sleep, the longest of his career.

His time was winding down. He had received reports, good ones, concerning the temperament of his successor, an impatient sort of person free of any noticeable bias on behalf of equality or federal assistance, or anything thereto related. Reports suggested that he had already killed his man, an English professor it was said, who imagined he could reprimand The Successor in the open streets. But was he prepared, this young new leader, to sway The Council and form policies for the better half (in both senses) of the then-known world? Yes, actually he was.

In September the following year Reuben mustered The Council, a much larger organization now with 143 members representing European constituencies mostly, for what in retrospect was surely the most crucial debate of the twenty-first century. Still disappointed in the behavior of unsupervised humans when they thought they weren't being seen; disappointed, too, in their reading matter; disappointed especially in their tendency to come together in cities and speak to one another; and disappointed above all in their bodily actualities, their fluids and fluttering eyes, their secretions and "reproductive" equipment. Disappointed in this and just about everything else as well, he persuaded The Council with only two demurrals to divert a half-*trillion* dollars into an emergency search for life forms that might be nobler than the ones already too well known. Space, of course, was much deeper than generally believed, the opportunities greater, and meantime technology had advanced to such a level that even Reuben couldn't understand it.

Because of this, not two weeks had gone by before one of his favorite cosmologists had put himself into contact with a life form in the "Octopus" constellation some million-and-a-half light years from earth. Already overburdened with responsibilities, Reuben right away sent forward a message to his foreign minister requiring that this particular civilization be forever blocked from all places illuminated by our own custodial sun.

It was almost the last important decision of his administration. Sensing that he was in danger of lapsing intellectually to a level achievable by ordinary geniuses, he began to cast about for a place of retirement. His poverty gave him but few choices certainly; even so, he was intrigued by a gift from one of his constituents of four-and-a-half acres in the neighborhood of Port Sheridan, said also to include a three-room cabin in reasonable condition. He examined the place minutely on his escrubilator and convinced that the offer wasn't intended as an insult, drafted a reply in his best prose to the donor. Of course, he wrote as well to his successor, offering his advice and benediction, and entreating the man to follow along in his own trajectory. He also offered his big black dog, his tiara, a set of brass knuckles for the right hand, and his own worn copy of Cockayne's *Leechdoms, Wortcunning, and Star Craft.*

Finally, with winter threatening, he set out from Dafter, a largish town in northern Michigan, and on that first afternoon covered six miles before settling in for the night in a concrete culvert obstructed with spider webs. His leg was not any better than of sixty years before; on the contrary it was worse. No flesh between the ankle and the knee, while the bone itself had become porous and visibly vermiculated owing to age. Insofar as he was able to see what he was doing in the dying light, he wrapped it in gauze and then shortly fell off into a REM sleep in which he imagined—his favorite dream—that he was dead already.

By noon on the second day he came within ken of Mackinac Island, a listless place, intellectually barren, whence he wheedled a fisherman to row him across to Canada proper. Began now his ordeal in truth. The ground was flat, the cities tiny, and the few persons he met were as likely to recognize him as if he had accomplished nothing in his own country. Three days ago his writ had run as far as he could see, but not now, now that he was constantly pelted by small boys who made it quite impossible to do any serious reading while on the march. And then, too, he had allocated himself just $25, and two of these were already gone. (He had bought a soft drink and, for nostalgia's sake, a certain out-of-date candy bar that turned to rubble even as he took it from its wrapper.) Unwilling to turn back and repeat the intervening miles in order to claim a refund, he turned east at the juncture of highway 17 and a narrow pathway with a great many potholes in it. And yet he was moving forward rather efficiently, never mind the thirty pounds of books and comestibles that he carried in a knapsack. His timepiece he had left behind.

Followed then sixty-two days in silence as he detoured around Indian settlements and crevasses, sometime running up against bays and lakes of which there were a very great many. He *had* brought fishing tackle, but had alas lost much of it in the mouths of the enormous sturgeons that frequented these northern waters. He saw herds of moose but no longer had the strength to chase them down. Finally, worst of all, he lost his .357 Smith and Wesson eight-shot revolver as he was taking a drink from a swiftly flowing river named in honor of himself.

Of course, he knew nothing of this, nor the names of the other physical features that came up to meet him on that snow-burdened scene. On Tuesday he passed under the brow of a hill with a cone-shaped fortification on the summit, three discrete faces visible in the windows. Except for that, he was not bothered by anyone, not till he limped into a wretched little hamlet offering supplies for hunters and fishermen and people like him. At once Reuben spread his cash out on the counter and asked the proprietor, a wrinkled man of poor genetic material, to fetch as many tins of beans and meat and bottles of rum as that amount of money could buy. Obviously, he could have slain the man on the spot, could have Reuben, had not his predisposition for such action more or less abandoned him over the last recent weeks.

And now he had no money at all, the same amount precisely as on that day he had intruded upon Leland's attention and wheedled the man out of a glass of water. Water? There was enough of that in his immediate environs to satisfy every legitimate thirst in the entire hemisphere.

On Friday he saw a bear, but neither of them could catch the other. He did succeed after much trouble in running down one of the cubs, a portly creature who supplied Reuben with the makings of a pair of fur-lined gloves and three days of a dark rich meat better than beef. After that he continued on, reaching the age of sixty-one at the same moment he came up over a hill and saw what lay in front of him.

Thirty-six

Almost no information has come down to us regarding his stay on Ellesmere Island, save that he did reach the place in middle November before the very worst of the weather would have cut off all access to the place. The storekeeper in Alert remembered him only as a large man in a sealskin coat and moccasins of polar bear fur. Apparently, he had offered to trade an autographed book for a box of matches, a pound of coffee, and a quart of turpentine, an arrangement the shopkeeper feared to refuse owing to the stranger's manner and size.

As to the condition of his hut when finally he found it on the extreme eastern boundary of his four-and-a-half-acre plot—no one has claimed to know anything about that. Later on, of course, when photographs of that rather pathetic dwelling were featured on two highly *recherché* sets of Russian and European postage stamps (air travel to the location having by then been regularized for the tourist trade), *then* it could be seen how few really were his possessions—a chair, table, writing desk, and half-finished manuscript, almost illegible, in which the boy had tried to justify himself to his mentor.

His remains were never found, neither in the house nor yet in the outlying steppes, nor even indeed along the shore of the sea. It formed a mystery that for a few weeks at least excited a certain curiosity among civilized people.

ABOUT THE AUTHOR

Tito Perdue was born in 1938 in Chile, the son of an electrical engineer from Alabama. The family returned to Alabama in 1941, where Tito graduated from the Indian Springs School, a private academy near Birmingham, in 1956. He then attended Antioch College in Ohio for a year, before being expelled for cohabitating with a female student, Judy Clark. In 1957, they were married, and remain so today. He graduated from the University of Texas in 1961, and spent some time working in New York City, an experience which garnered him his life-long hatred of urban life. After holding positions at various university libraries, Tito has devoted himself full-time to writing since 1983.

His first novel, 1991's *Lee*, received favorable reviews in *The New York Times*, *The Los Angeles Reader*, and *The New England Review of Books*. In addition to the present volume, his novels include *The New Austerities* (1994), *Opportunities in Alabama Agriculture* (1994), *The Sweet-Scented Manuscript* (2004), *Fields of Asphodel* (2007), *The Node* (2011), *Morning Crafts* (2013), the *William's House* quartet (2016), *Cynosura* (2017), *Philip* (2017), *Though We Be Dead, Yet Our Day Will Come* (2018), *The Bent Pyramid* (2018), *The Philatelist* (2018), *The Smut Book* (2018), *The Gizmo* (2019), *Love Song of the Australopiths* (2020), *Materials for All Future Historians* (2020), *Journey to a Location* (2021), and *Vade Mecum* (2021)—which have been praised in *Chronicles*, *The Quarterly Review*, *The Occidental Observer*, and *Counter-Currents*.

In 2015, he received the H. P. Lovecraft Prize for Literature.